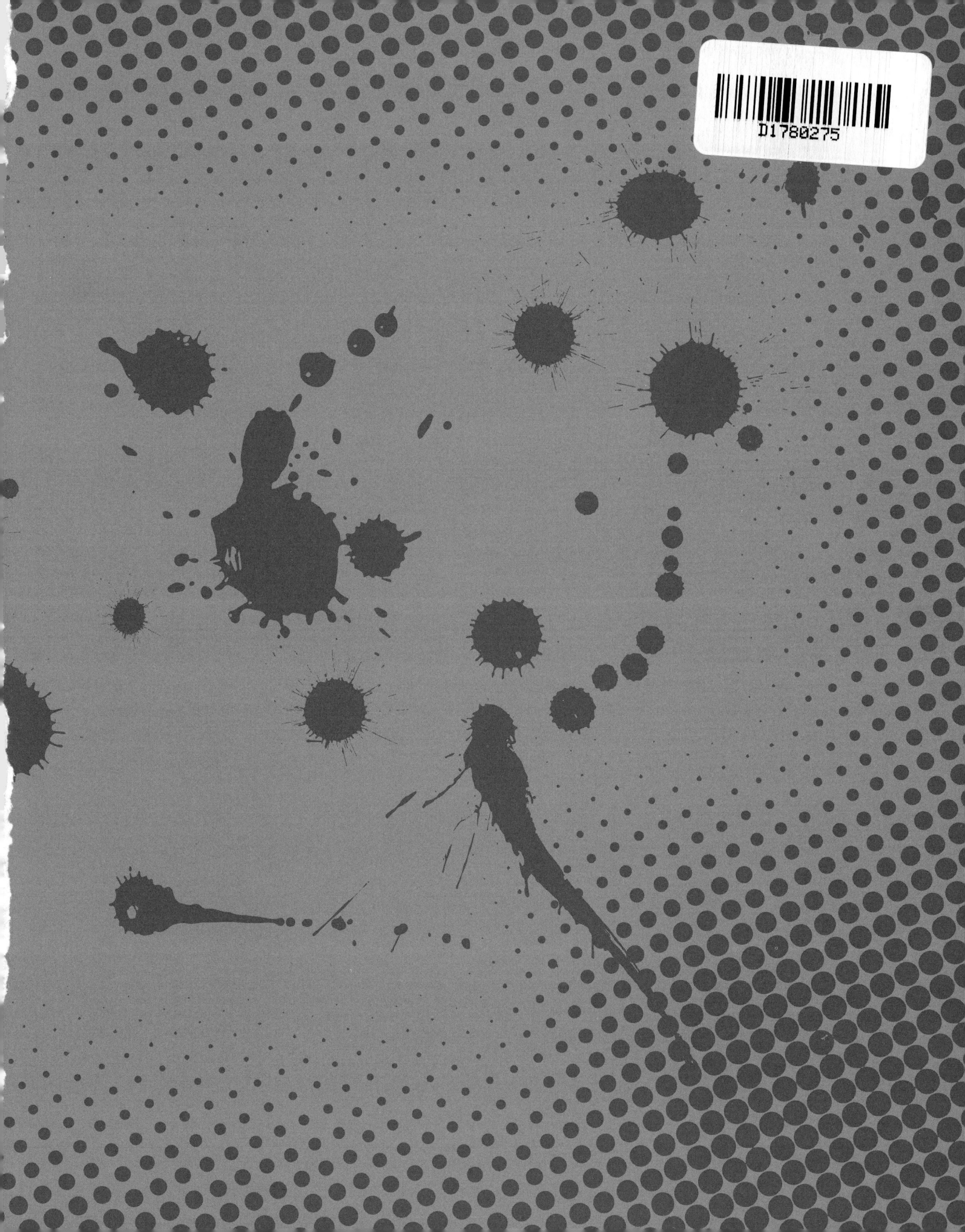

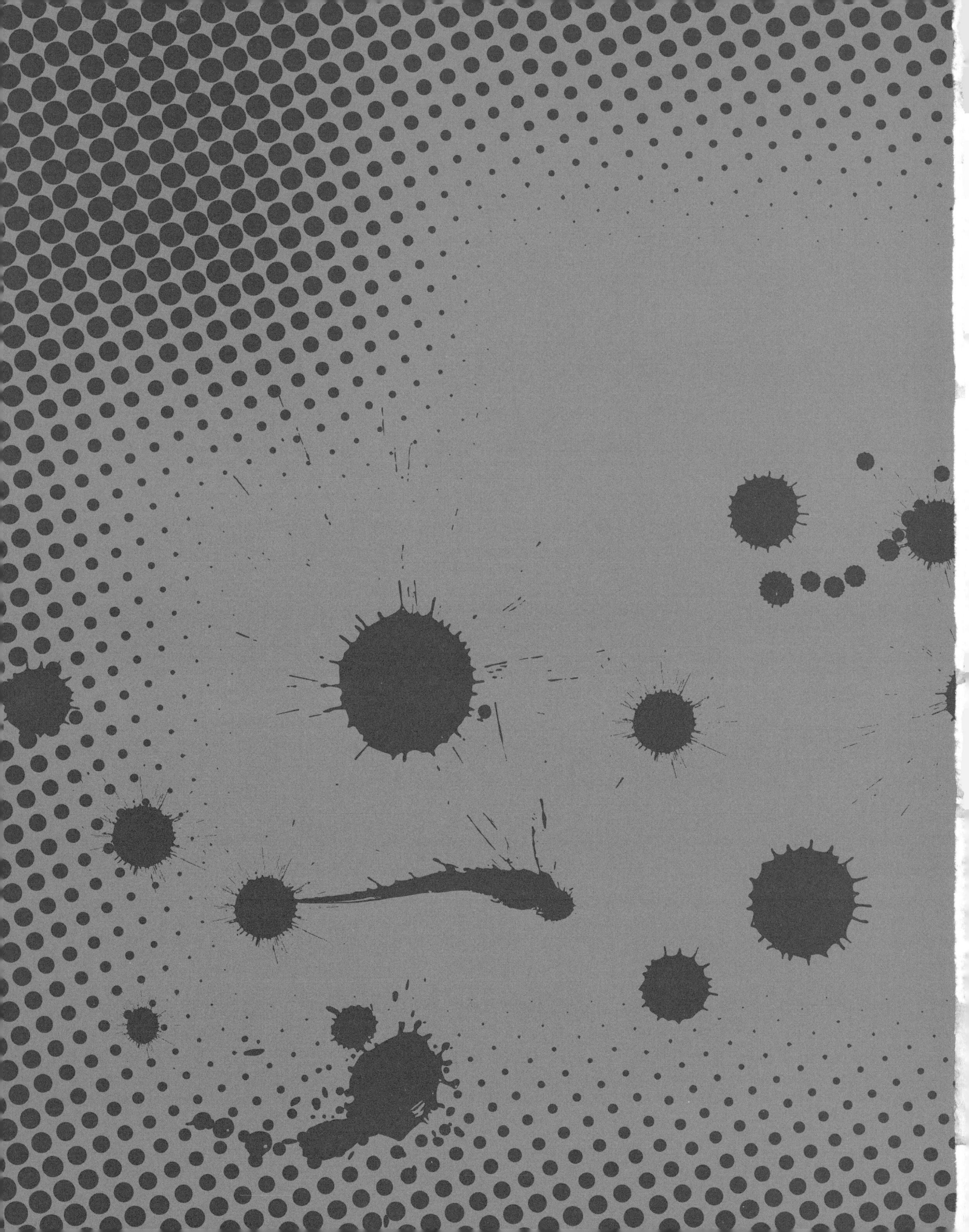

INSIDER'S ENCYCLOPEDIA

EVERYTHING YOU NEED TO KNOW

Silver Dolphin Books
An imprint of Printers Row Publishing Group
A division of Readerlink Distribution Services, LLC
10350 Barnes Canyon Road, Suite 100, San Diego, CA 92121
www.silverdolphinbooks.com

Copyright 2019 © Discovery Communications, LLC. Discovery™ and the Discovery™ logo are trademarks of Discovery Communications, LLC, used under license.

All rights reserved. No part of this publication may be reproduced, distributed, or transmitted in any form or by any means, including photocopying, recording, or other electronic or mechanical methods, without the prior written permission of the publisher, except in the case of brief quotations embodied in critical reviews and certain other noncommercial uses permitted by copyright law.

Printers Row Publishing Group is a division of Readerlink Distribution Services, LLC.
Silver Dolphin Books is a registered trademark of Readerlink Distribution Services, LLC.

All notations of errors or omissions should be addressed to Silver Dolphin Books, Editorial Department, at the above address.

ISBN: 978-1-68412-900-3

Manufactured, printed, and assembled in Heshan, China.
LP/10/19
23 22 21 20 19   1 2 3 4 5

Written by Sheila Sweeny Higginson & Clyde Bosco
Consultants: Dr. Alex Peroff & Beth Adelman

Interiors designed, produced, and packaged by Big Yellow Taxi, Inc.

INSIDER'S ENCYCLOPEDIA

EVERYTHING YOU NEED TO KNOW

Silver Dolphin

CONTENTS

OUTER SPACE AND PLANET EARTH

You Are Here 6
Here Comes the Sun 8
Welcome to the Neighborhood 10
Earth's Moon 12
Little Blue Pool 14
Rock On! 16
Smash Hit 18
Blast Off! 20
Danger in Orbit 22

NATURE

There's No Place Like Home! 24
Old-Timers 26
Rings of Time 28
Denizens of the Deep 30
Wild Eyes 32
Warning! 34
Chomp! 36
Sky High 38
Animals Count 40
Colossal Creepers 42
Smarts and Skills 44

THE HUMAN BODY

Human Bodies: By the Numbers 46
Pieces of You 48
Bones 50
Drop by Drop 52
The Outside Story 54
Hair and Now 56
Brains! 58
Wild Comparisons 60

SCIENCE AND TECHNOLOGY

Discover the Past 62
Viewfinder 64
In the Toolbox 66
History's Mysteries 68
Home Sweet Home 70
Going Up 72
Wow in the World! 74
On the Road 76
How Low Can You Go? 78
Incredible Crossings 80
Ride the Rails 82
In the Driver's Seat 84
High Flyers 86
Up, Up, and Away 88
Survival Suits 90
Processing Power 92
Phone Fever 94
Here Come the Robots 96

HISTORY AND CIVILIZATIONS

Maps 98
Same World, Different Views 100
Waving the Flag 102
On the Money 104
Name That Country 106
Election Day 108
City Starters 110
The X Factor 112

WORDS AND LANGUAGE

Everybody's Talking	146
You Don't Say!	148
Top Secret!	150
Hieroglyphs	152
My Word!	154
What's in a Name?	156
Quite a Mouthful!	158
Terms of Terror	160
Part of the Team	162
Cover Up!	164

TOYS, GAMES, AND SPORTS

Let's Play!	188
Bits and Pieces	190
Stuffed!	192
Blocked!	194
Sport Rules!	196
Goofy Greatness	198
Whack!	200
Rule Breakers	202
Weird World of Sports	204

ARTS AND ENTERTAINMENT

Cave Paintings	114
The Masterpiece	116
Celebrated Styles	118
The Music Makers	120
Extraordinary Notes	122
Fashion Forward	124
These Shoes Are Made for Walking	126
Hats Off to . . . HATS!	128
That's Entertainment!	130
A Round of Applause	132
It's Crowded in Here	134
Dance With Me	136
A Walk in the Park	138
Mark That Date!	140
Funfest	142
There's a Museum for That?	144

FOOD

Hot, Hot, Hot!	166
Snack Time!	168
You Scream, I Scream	170
How Sweet It Is!	172
Fresh!	174
Griddle Me This	176
Order Up!	178
Season's Greetings	180
Secret Ingredients	182
Global Gourmets	184
Table Talk	186

COMPARISONS

What Are the Odds?	206
Up in the Air	208
Hit the Road	210
Growing Up	212
Is It Hot in Here?	214
Dare to Compare	216

OUTER SPACE AND PLANET EARTH

You Are Here

OUR PLACE IN THE MILKY WAY GALAXY

You and everyone you know lives in the Milky Way galaxy.

Galaxies are groups of billions of stars held together by gravity. The Milky Way is a barred spiral galaxy, shaped like a disk, with "arms" made of stars.

One of those stars is particularly important to us: the Sun. It is located about two-thirds of the way from the center of the galaxy. Without it, life on Earth wouldn't be possible!

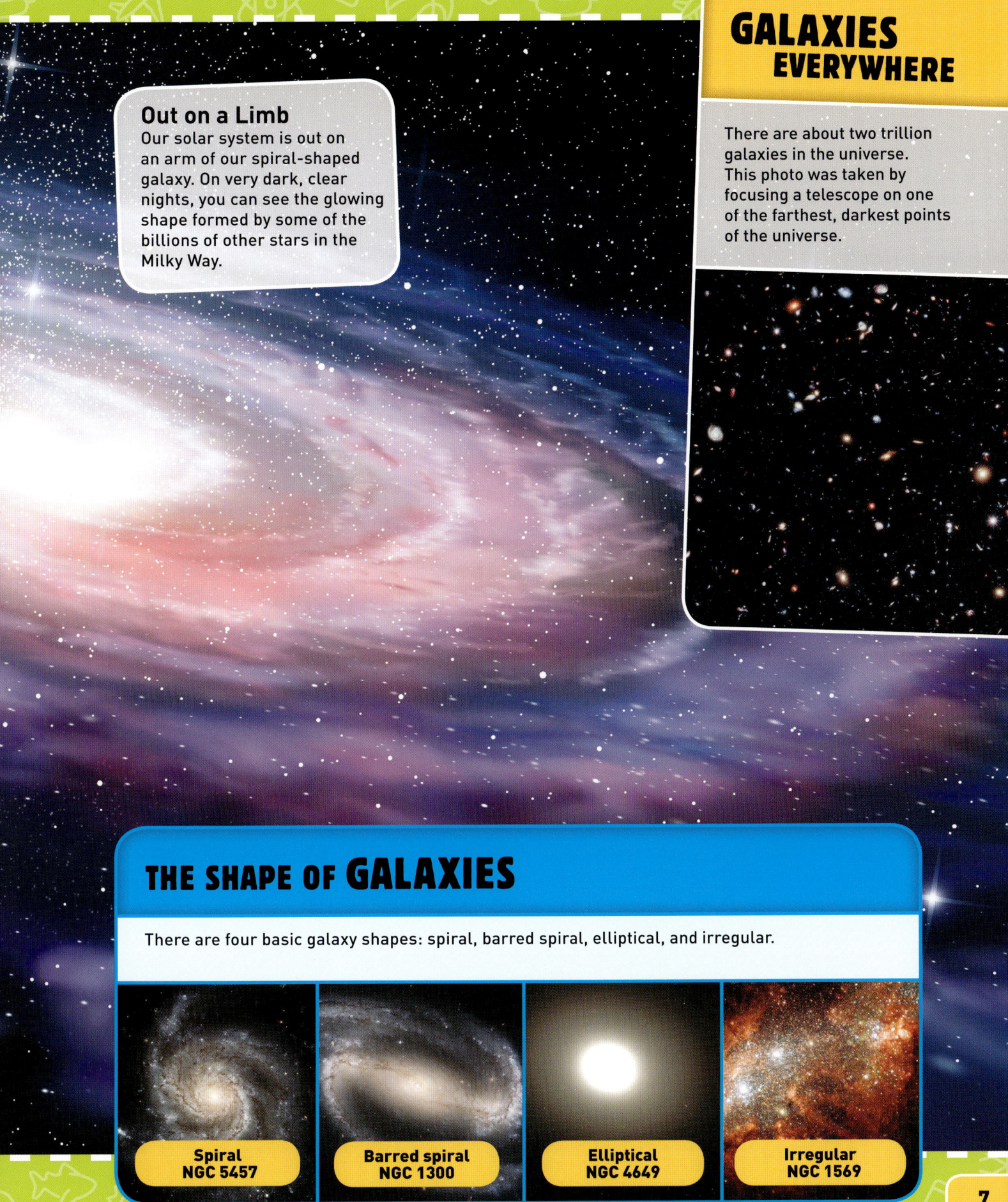

GALAXIES EVERYWHERE

There are about two trillion galaxies in the universe. This photo was taken by focusing a telescope on one of the farthest, darkest points of the universe.

Out on a Limb
Our solar system is out on an arm of our spiral-shaped galaxy. On very dark, clear nights, you can see the glowing shape formed by some of the billions of other stars in the Milky Way.

THE SHAPE OF GALAXIES

There are four basic galaxy shapes: spiral, barred spiral, elliptical, and irregular.

- **Spiral** NGC 5457
- **Barred spiral** NGC 1300
- **Elliptical** NGC 4649
- **Irregular** NGC 1569

OUTER SPACE AND PLANET EARTH

Here Comes the Sun

THE STAR OF THE SOLAR SYSTEM

The Sun is a blazing ball of superheated gas. The force of gravity pulls together the Sun's materials, causing atoms to smash together, releasing energy. This process is called fusion. It sends light and heat out to the solar system, warming and powering life on Earth.

Corona
The Sun's outer atmosphere, the corona, reaches millions of miles into space, with temperatures of about 900,000 degrees Fahrenheit (500,000 degrees Celsius), although it can get even hotter.

Chromosphere
This is the inner layer of the Sun's atmosphere. Temperatures closer to the Sun's core are around 6,700 degrees Fahrenheit (3,700 degrees Celsuis) and reach 14,000 degrees Fahrenheit (7,700 degrees Celsius) as you go farther out.

Photosphere
This is the deepest part of the Sun that we can see. The temperature is about 10,800 degrees Fahrenheit (6,000 degrees Celsius).

Convection Zone
This area carries energy upward through columns of hot gas.

Radiation Zone
This layer moves energy fron the core outward through the Sun.

Core
The Sun's core is about 27,000,000 degrees Fahrenheit (15,000,000 degrees Celsius).

SUNSPOTS

Sunspots, the dark shapes that appear on the photosphere, are caused by patches of gas that are thousands of degrees cooler than the rest of the surface.

OUTER SPACE AND PLANET EARTH

Welcome to the Neighborhood

EARTH IS IN JUST THE RIGHT SPOT

Eight planets orbit the Sun, along with hundreds of thousands of other objects, such as comets, asteroids, and dwarf planets.

The four planets closest to the Sun have solid surfaces. This makes them terrestrial planets. The other ones are huge balls of gas. They are called the Jovian planets, or the gas giants.

Mercury
Closest to the Sun, Mercury is a ball of rock covered with craters.

Venus
About the same size as the Earth, Venus is a hot and dangerous world, covered by clouds of acid.

Mars
Often called "The Red Planet," Mars is covered with iron oxide dust. In the past, there may have been liquid water on the surface. There is ice on the surface, and it's possible that there may still be water underground.

Earth
Our home planet orbits the Sun at just the right distance, known as "The Goldilocks Zone." It's not so close to the Sun that water evaporates and not so far that all the water freezes.

THE ASTEROID BELT

A ring of asteroids—pieces of rock and metal—orbit the Sun between Jupiter and Mars. Scientists think asteroids may be material that would have been pulled into a newly forming planet, but the gravity from Jupiter kept them from coming together.

Jupiter
Jupiter is the largest planet, and has twice the material of all the other planets combined. It's a huge ball of hydrogen and helium gas, with a giant red spot—a huge storm that is hundreds of years old.

Neptune
The eighth planet is 30 times farther from the Sun than the Earth is. Neptune appears bright blue, due to methane gas in its atmosphere.

Saturn
Like Jupiter, Saturn is a huge ball of gas. It is best known for its amazing rings, formed from billions of pieces of ice and rock.

Uranus
Uranus rotates sideways; one of its poles is always facing the Sun. It is so far away from the Sun that it takes 84 Earth years for Uranus to complete one orbit.

OUTER SPACE AND PLANET EARTH

Earth's Moon
OUR SPECIAL SATELLITE

The Moon is brighter and larger than anything else in the night sky. That's because it is, by far, the closest to the Earth of any object in space.

Orbiting at 238,855 miles (384,400 kilometers) away, the Moon is Earth's constant companion. Our closest neighboring planet is Venus, approximately 26 million miles (41,887,000 kilometers) away.

The Moon is about a quarter of the size of the Earth. As its gravity pulls on the Earth's surface, it causes tides.

BORN WITH A BANG

Many scientists believe the Moon was created when, about 4.5 billion years ago, a rock the size of Mars crashed into the Earth.

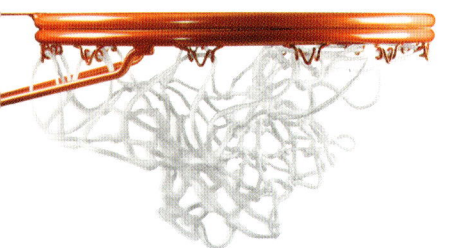

FUN FACT!

On the Moon, gravity is only 17 percent of Earth's gravity, and you would be able to jump about 11 times higher than you normally do. Imagine how easy it would be to slam-dunk!

ECLIPSES

Eclipses occur when the Moon, Sun, and Earth are in a straight line. A lunar eclipse happens when the Earth is between the Sun and Moon. A solar eclipse happens when the Moon gets between the Sun and Earth.

PERMANENT PRINTS

There is no wind on the Moon, so an astronaut's footprints will stay undisturbed for centuries!

CRATERS

The Moon's surface is covered with craters because it was hit by so many space rocks while the solar system was still forming, about four billion years ago.

OUTER SPACE AND PLANET EARTH

Little Blue Pool

EARTH IS THE WATER PLANET

Seventy percent of the Earth's surface is covered with water. This gives our planet its blue color when seen from space. Water also exists under the ground and in the air. It is the main reason that life can exist here at all.

The liquid part of the Earth is called the hydrosphere. It includes oceans, lakes, rivers, water in the air and underground, snow, and ice.

ICE, BABY!

About 75 percent of the Earth's fresh water is frozen in glaciers—the source of icebergs like this one.

LIFE AND TIMES

Over the course of 100 years, a water molecule spends 98 years in the ocean, 20 months as ice, about two weeks in rivers and lakes, and less than a week in the atmosphere.

DID YOU KNOW?

Only 2.5 percent of all the water on Earth is fresh water that can be used by the living things on our planet, and about 1 percent of that is easy to get to. The rest is mostly frozen.

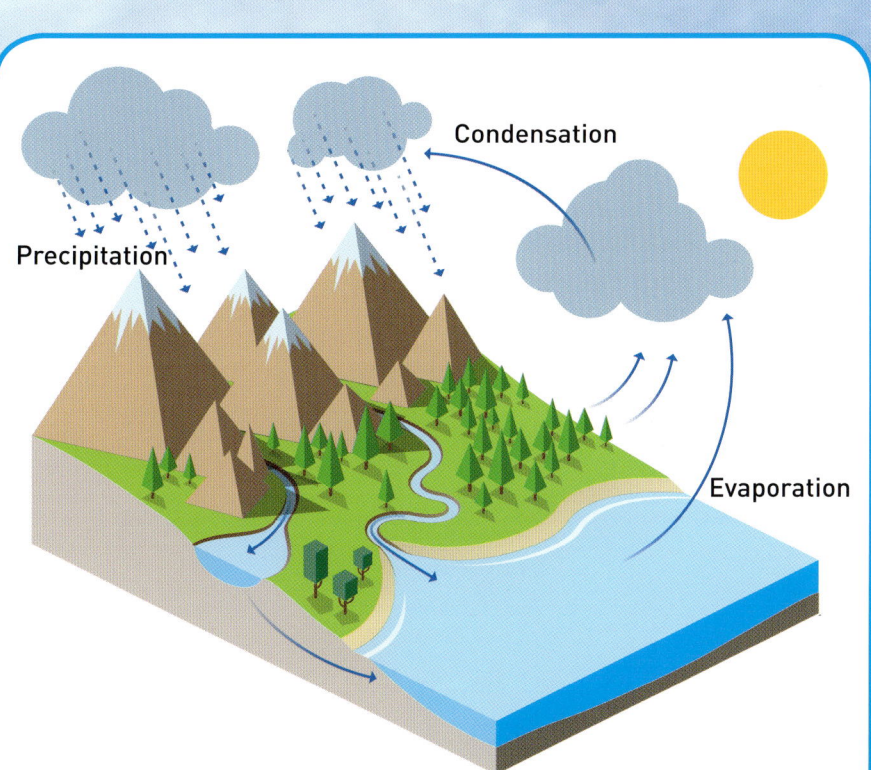

KEEP MOVING!

Water moves around the Earth in a cycle. The main three parts of this water cycle are evaporation, condensation, and precipitation.

OUTER SPACE AND PLANET EARTH

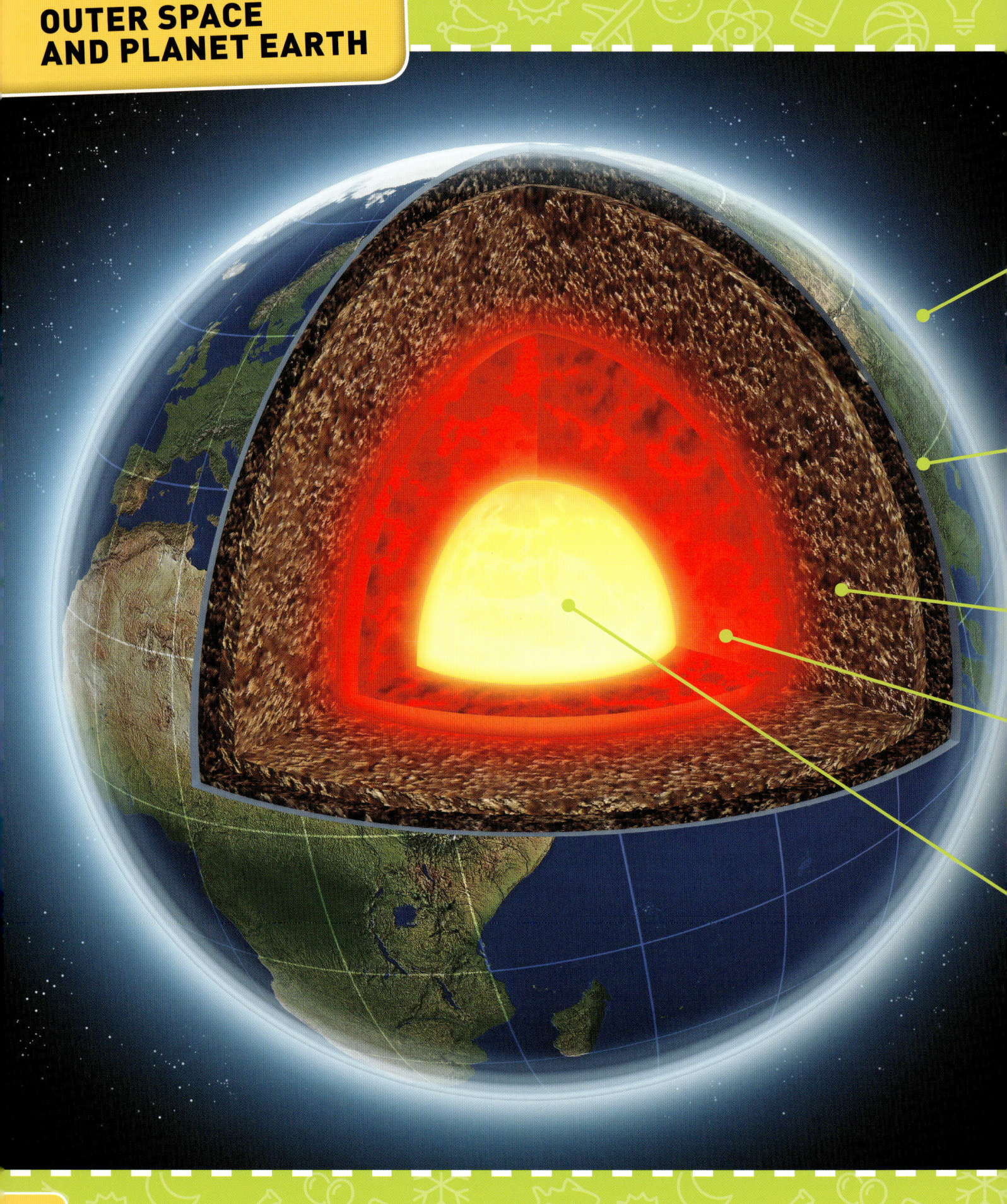

Rock On!

EARTH'S **SURFACE** AND **STRUCTURE**

In addition to water and gases, the Earth is made up of different layers of rock and metal in solid and liquid form.

The average distance from the surface to the center of the Earth is 3,959 miles (6,371 kilometers). Here's how thick each of the planet's layers are.

The Atmosphere
Earth's protective layer, reaching 300 miles (480 kilometers) above the surface, includes the air we breathe. Without the atmosphere, our planet would be peppered by meteorites and bathed in radiation.

The Lithosphere
You are here! The dry land is continental crust, which is about 5 miles (8 kilometers) to 43.5 miles (70 kilometers) thick. The layer of rock under the ocean bed is oceanic crust, and is about 5 miles (8 kilometers) thick.

The Mantle
A dense and hot layer of semi-solid rock that stretches 1,800 miles (2,897 kilometers) below the crust.

The Outer Core
This layer of liquid iron and nickel is about 3,200 miles (5,510 kilometers) deep. The movement of this layer causes Earth's magnetic fields.

The Inner Core
The center of the Earth is a ball of iron about 1,500 miles (2,500 kilometers) across. It's super hot, but is solid metal because of the intense pressure caused by everything around it.

SUNBLOCK

Earth's atmosphere stops 49 percent of solar radiation from reaching the surface.

OUTER SPACE AND PLANET EARTH

Smash Hit
OUR **PELTED** PLANET

The Earth is blasted with more than 100 tons (91 metric tons) of space material every day. Most of it burns up in the atmosphere, but occasionally, some pieces of metal and rock get through!

Meteor Crater is a crater in Arizona that was formed when a meteorite struck the Earth 50,000 years ago. It is 0.75 miles (1.2 kilometers) wide and 560 feet (171 meters) deep.

MONSTER MASH

The Hoba Meteorite fell in Namibia about 80,000 years ago. It is an enormous 66-ton (60-metric ton) rock and has been declared a national monument.

18

THE CULPRIT (PART OF IT)

The Holsinger Meteorite is a fragment of the object that caused Meteor Crater. The complete meteorite was 150 feet (45 meters) across.

THE DINOSAURS' REALLY BAD DAY!

Some scientists think a comet struck the Earth 65 million years ago, putting an end to the age of dinosaurs.

OUTER SPACE AND PLANET EARTH

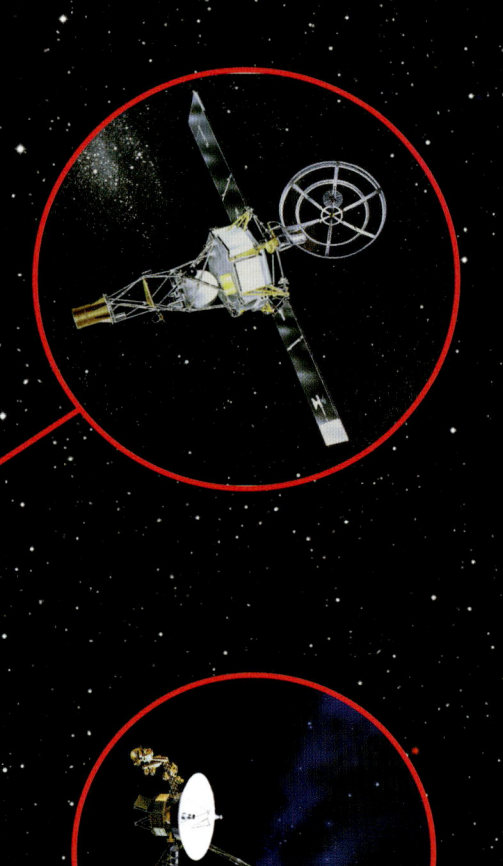

Sputnik
In 1957, the Russian satellite became the first artificial satellite to orbit the Earth.

Mariner 2
In 1962, it flew by Venus, giving humanity its first encounter with another planet.

Viking 1 and Viking 2
In 1976, *Viking 1* and *Viking 2* landed and sent back the first pictures of Mars' surface.

Voyager 2
Launched in 1977, it flew by Jupiter, Saturn, Uranus, and Neptune.

Mars Pathfinder
In 1997, it was the first robotic mission to travel around the surface of the Red Planet.

Messenger
In 2011, it first orbited Mercury.

Chandrayaan 1
In 2008, India's first lunar probe orbited and then (intentionally) crashed into the Moon . . . and discovered water.

FIRST ONE OUT

Launched in 1977, *Voyager 1* became, on August 25, 2012, the first human-made object to exit the solar system.

Blast Off!

HUMANS EXPLORE THE SOLAR SYSTEM

Humans have left the Earth and walked on the Moon. Scientists are working on missions that might send people to Mars in your lifetime. Meanwhile, robots and satellites have been busy exploring the solar system and beyond!

OUTER SPACE AND PLANET EARTH

Danger in Orbit

TRAVELING THROUGH SPACE JUNK

TRACKING TRASH

To prevent collisions, the Space Surveillance Network tracks more than 20,000 of the largest objects orbiting the Earth.

Spacecraft that no longer work, abandoned launch vehicle stages, and bits of satellites and instruments are among the millions of pieces of human-made space junk that orbit the Earth.

There are about 500,000 pieces of debris the size of a marble or larger. More than 20,000 of them are the size of a softball or larger.

DID YOU KNOW?

Items in orbit travel up to 17,500 miles (28,164 kilometers) per hour. Even a tiny bolt or screw could cause critical damage if it hit a satellite or space vehicle.

SPACE TRASH

- Garbage bags jettisoned from the *Mir* space station
- A camera dropped by an astronaut during a spacewalk
- Thousands of parts of a satellite blown up in a weapons test
- Leftover pieces of rocket boosters

SKY CRASH

So far, there have been only a few collisions in space, but each one makes even more space garbage. In 2009, two satellites crashed into each other, creating 2,000 pieces of space junk.

NATURE

There's No Place Like Home!

LIFE IN **EXTREME** ENVIRONMENTS

As special and habitable as our planet is, there are some places where it seems impossible that anything could survive. Incredibly, some creatures can thrive in some of the harshest locations on the planet.

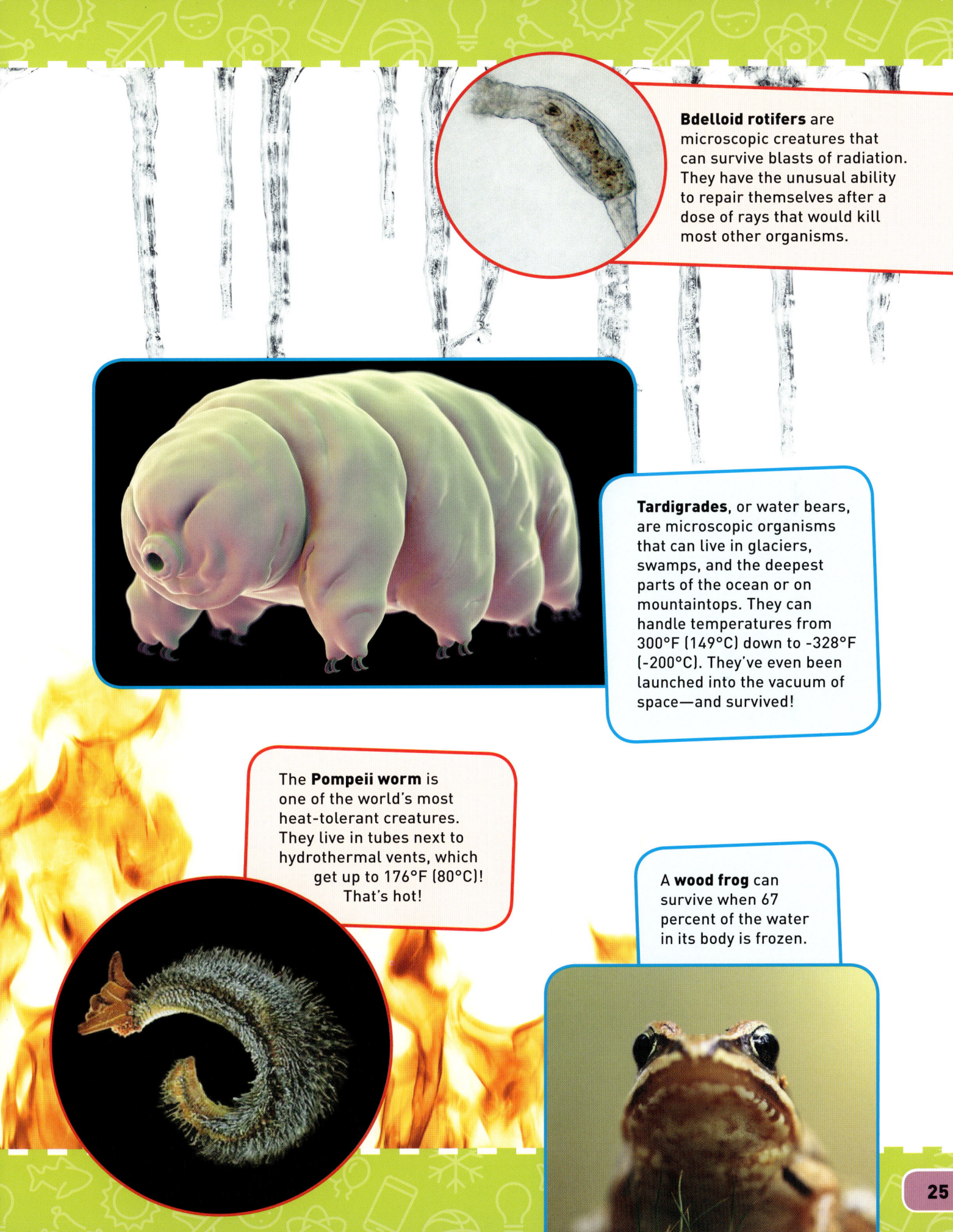

Bdelloid rotifers are microscopic creatures that can survive blasts of radiation. They have the unusual ability to repair themselves after a dose of rays that would kill most other organisms.

Tardigrades, or water bears, are microscopic organisms that can live in glaciers, swamps, and the deepest parts of the ocean or on mountaintops. They can handle temperatures from 300°F (149°C) down to -328°F (-200°C). They've even been launched into the vacuum of space—and survived!

The **Pompeii worm** is one of the world's most heat-tolerant creatures. They live in tubes next to hydrothermal vents, which get up to 176°F (80°C)! That's hot!

A **wood frog** can survive when 67 percent of the water in its body is frozen.

NATURE

Giant barrel sponges can live more than 2,000 years.

Old-Timers

CALLING EARTH HOME FOR A LONG, **LONG TIME!**

The **longest-living human** was Jeanne Calment, who lived to the age of 122 years, 164 days.

Here's a salute to some of the planet's senior citizens: the oldest and longest-living things on Earth.

Aldabra giant tortoises are found in the Seychelles. They can live more than 200 years.

A sacred **fig tree** was planted in Anuradhapura, Sri Lanka, in 288 BCE. It is the oldest known human-planted tree in the world.

A **Great Basin bristlecone pine tree** in Utah is around 5,000 years old. It is the oldest known living thing on Earth.

NATURE

Rings of Time

MARKING HISTORY IN THE RINGS OF A TREE

By counting the rings of a cut tree, you can tell how old it is. Each ring shows one year of growth.

Since giant trees live for centuries, you can chart time in a cross section of a tree.

1564
William Shakespeare is born.

1973
The first mobile phone call

1861
The start of the Civil War

NATURE

Denizens of the Deep

AWESOME CREATURES FOUND UNDER THE SEA

More than 1,000 feet (305 meters) down— farther than any scuba diver has ever swum— amazing creatures make their way through the dimly lit depths.

Wolffish

Pacific Viperfish

Fangtooth Fish

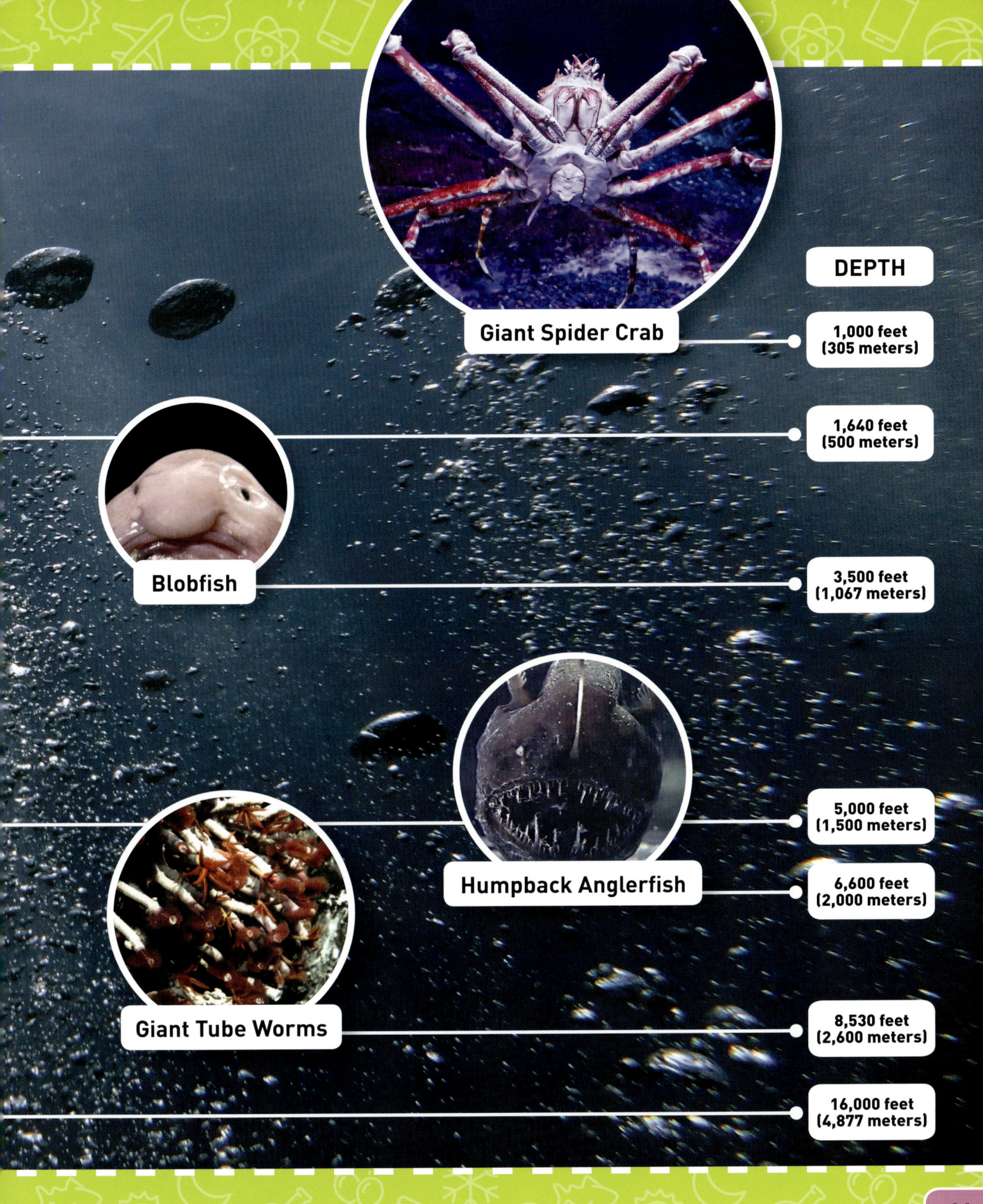

DEPTH

Giant Spider Crab — 1,000 feet (305 meters)

1,640 feet (500 meters)

Blobfish — 3,500 feet (1,067 meters)

Humpback Anglerfish — 5,000 feet (1,500 meters)

6,600 feet (2,000 meters)

Giant Tube Worms — 8,530 feet (2,600 meters)

16,000 feet (4,877 meters)

NATURE

An **eagle's** eyes can weigh more than its brain!

The **scallop** has 100 eyes around the edge of its shell. They help detect the shadows of approaching predators.

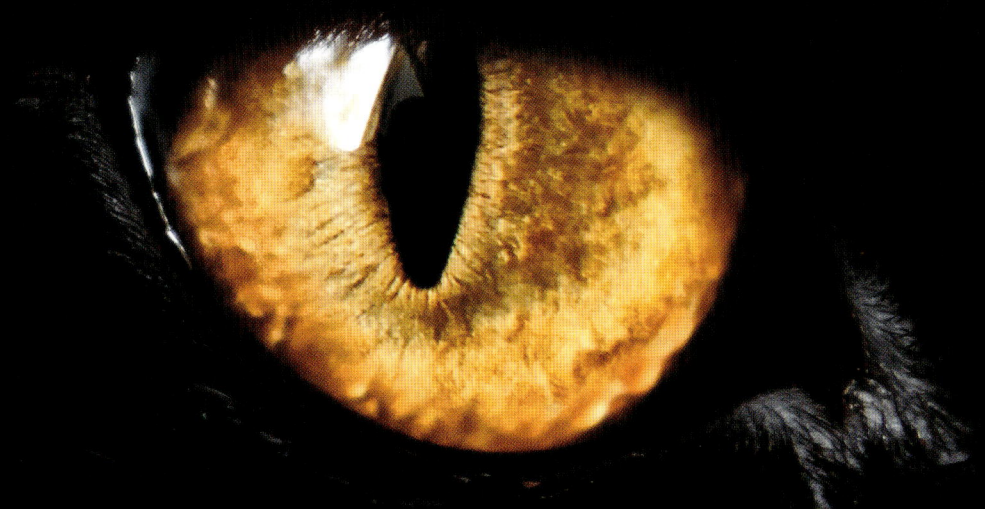

Cats' eyes are designed for hunting. Cats have excellent night vision, and they are good at sensing sudden movements.

Wild Eyes
ANIMALS ON THE LOOKOUT

Animal eyes are different from human eyes. They are adapted to help animals in their world.

Insects have compound eyes with thousands of tiny lenses, so they can see danger coming from all directions.

A **crab's** eyes are on the ends of stalks. These stick up when the crab is buried.

A **snail's** eyes are on the ends of tentacles, so a snail can look around faster than it can turn around.

NATURE

Warning!
THESE ANIMALS ARE VENOMOUS!

Animals use deadly venom to eat—and to keep from being eaten. Here are some dangerous facts about nature's deadly creatures.

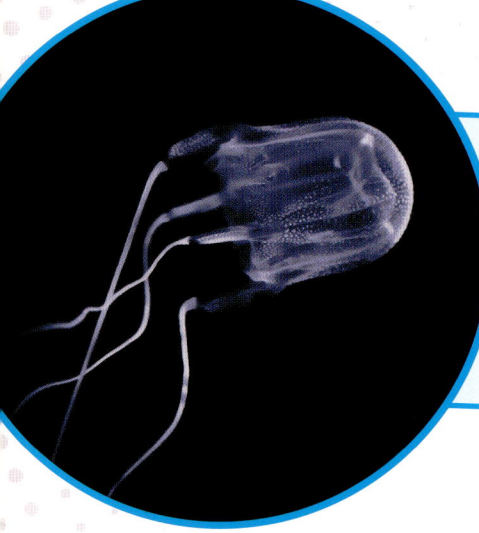

Box jellyfish are the most deadly venomous animals in the world. Each year, there are around 100 human deaths from box jellyfish stings.

Belcher's sea snakes have some of the most concentrated venom of all snakes, but they rarely use it, injecting venom into only 25 percent of people bitten.

Found in the Pacific and Indian Oceans, **stonefish** have 13 venomous spines that can cause paralysis and death to unlucky divers.

Deathstalker scorpions can be found in North Africa and the Middle East. Their sting can cause pain, paralysis, and death.

This tiny, golf ball–sized **blue-ringed octopus** carries enough poison to kill 26 humans. There is no known antidote.

NATURE

Also called a sundew, the **Drosera** has sticky tentacles that glue prey in place while the plant closes and feasts.

Chomp!
PLANTS **BITE** BACK

Some plants turn the tables on insects. Here are some carnivorous plants that eat instead of being eaten.

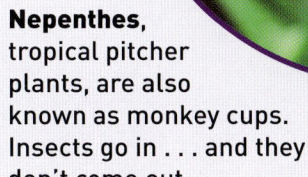

Nepenthes, tropical pitcher plants, are also known as monkey cups. Insects go in . . . and they don't come out.

When insects land on the floating **waterwheel plant**, its arms quickly fold around them. It's sometimes called a snap trap.

Hinged leaves close on flies and other creatures that make the mistake of landing on the **Venus flytrap**. Its leaves seal around the prey and act like a plant stomach.

Sarracenia, also known as trumpet pitcher plants, lure insects into their cuplike bodies, where the bugs fall in, die, and get digested.

NATURE

Sky High

SOME ANIMALS MOVE IN SURPRISING WAYS

Here are some animals that defy expectations. These creatures aren't birds, bats, or bugs, yet they take to the sky.

The **Mobula,** or devil ray, is similar to a manta ray. It can grow up to 17 feet (5 meters) long, and it can leap several feet out of the water.

Wallace's flying frog lives in the treetops of Malaysia and Indonesia. Skin flaps between its long, webbed toes allow it to "parachute" down to the ground.

There are 43 species of **flying squirrels**. They leap from trees and glide through the air on flaps of skin that stretch between their limbs.

The **flying snake** lives in Asian rain forests and leaps from trees. It flattens its body to maximize its surface area and coast through the air.

There are 50 different species of **flying fish**. They leap from the water and use their fins as wings to glide for up to 45 seconds at a time.

NATURE

Animals Count

SOME **AMAZING** ANIMAL NUMBERS

An octopus has eight arms. That's an easy one. Here are some amazing numbers and stats of the animal kingdom.

There are more than 12,000 species of **ant**.

A beehive can be home to 80,000 **bees** at a time.

Adult **elephants** can eat between 200 and 600 pounds (91 and 272 kilograms) of food a day.

There are about 200 million **insects** for every human on Earth.

Hummingbirds can visit 2,000 flowers in a day for nectar.

Basket stars have five arms, like most starfish, but they branch out into 50 or more smaller arms.

A **sperm whale's** brain weighs 17 pounds (7.8 kilograms).

41

NATURE

The **Atlas moth** has a wingspan of up to 1 foot (30 centimeters) across.

DRAGONS!

The largest insects that have ever lived were *Meganisoptera*, also known as griffinflies. They were giant, dragonfly-like creatures with a wingspan of more than 2 feet (61 centimeters) across! They lived more than 300 million years ago.

Colossal Creepers

BIG BUGS AND CRAWLY CRITTERS

Let's salute the biggest, heaviest, most massive creatures of the insect world.

Found in New Zealand, a **giant weta** is over 200 times the weight of a typical cricket!

At 3.5 ounces (99 grams), the **Goliath beetle** may be the heaviest insect on Earth today.

Found in the Amazon rain forest, the **titan beetle** can grow to be up to 6.6 inches (16.8 centimeters) long.

In Southeast Asia, some varieties of **giant walking sticks** can be 2 feet (61 centimeters) long.

NATURE

Parrots have been taught to count, sort shapes, and say 100 different words.

An **elephant** can recognize itself in a mirror.

Weaverbirds use 1,000 strands of grass to build a nest that is watertight and can hang from a tree branch.

Beavers can build a dam that completely changes the direction of a river.

Cathedral termites can build mounds that are 15 feet (4.6 meters) high.

Ants can tell other ants how to navigate a maze.

DID YOU KNOW?

Prairie dogs live in huge communities of underground burrows, called towns, which can stretch for miles. In Texas, a town of prairie dogs covering 25,000 square miles (64,750 square kilometers) was reported as the home to about 550 million prairie dogs.

Smarts and Skills

INDUSTRIOUS AND INTELLIGENT ANIMALS

Chimpanzees have been taught to understand about 3,000 English words.

THE HUMAN BODY

Human Bodies: By the Numbers

FACTS ABOUT YOUR BODY

Your body is a network of interconnected systems, all working together to keep you warm, fed, and alive. Here are some facts about amazing you.

In an average lifetime, a human's **heart** will beat about three billion times.

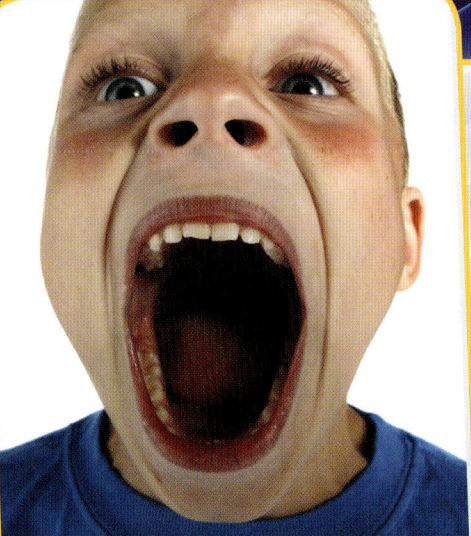

There are more bacteria in a person's **mouth** than there are people on planet Earth.

People **fart** about 14 times a day.

Every hour, a person sheds about 30,000 to 40,000 **skin cells**. That's about 1.5 pounds (0.7 kilograms) of skin a year.

FUN FACTS!

- You blink about 17 times per minute.
- That's 16,320 times per day (when you're not sleeping).
- That's six million times per year!

In a lifetime, a **human body** will process about 100,000 pounds (45,359 kilograms) of food.

As with fingerprints, every human has a unique **tongue print**.

Your **nose** and **ears** get larger as you age.

Over a lifetime, humans produce about 25,000 quarts (23,659 liters) of **saliva**. That's enough to fill two big swimming pools!

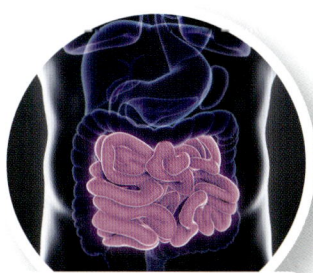

A person's **small intestine** can be about four times as long as their height.

A person takes about 23,000 **breaths** a day. That's around 673 million breaths in an average lifetime.

THE HUMAN BODY

Pieces of You

YOUR BODY IS MADE OF CELLS

All plants **and animals** are made of cells. Each cell has unique abilities, depending on the type of cell it is. Here are some awesome facts about cells.

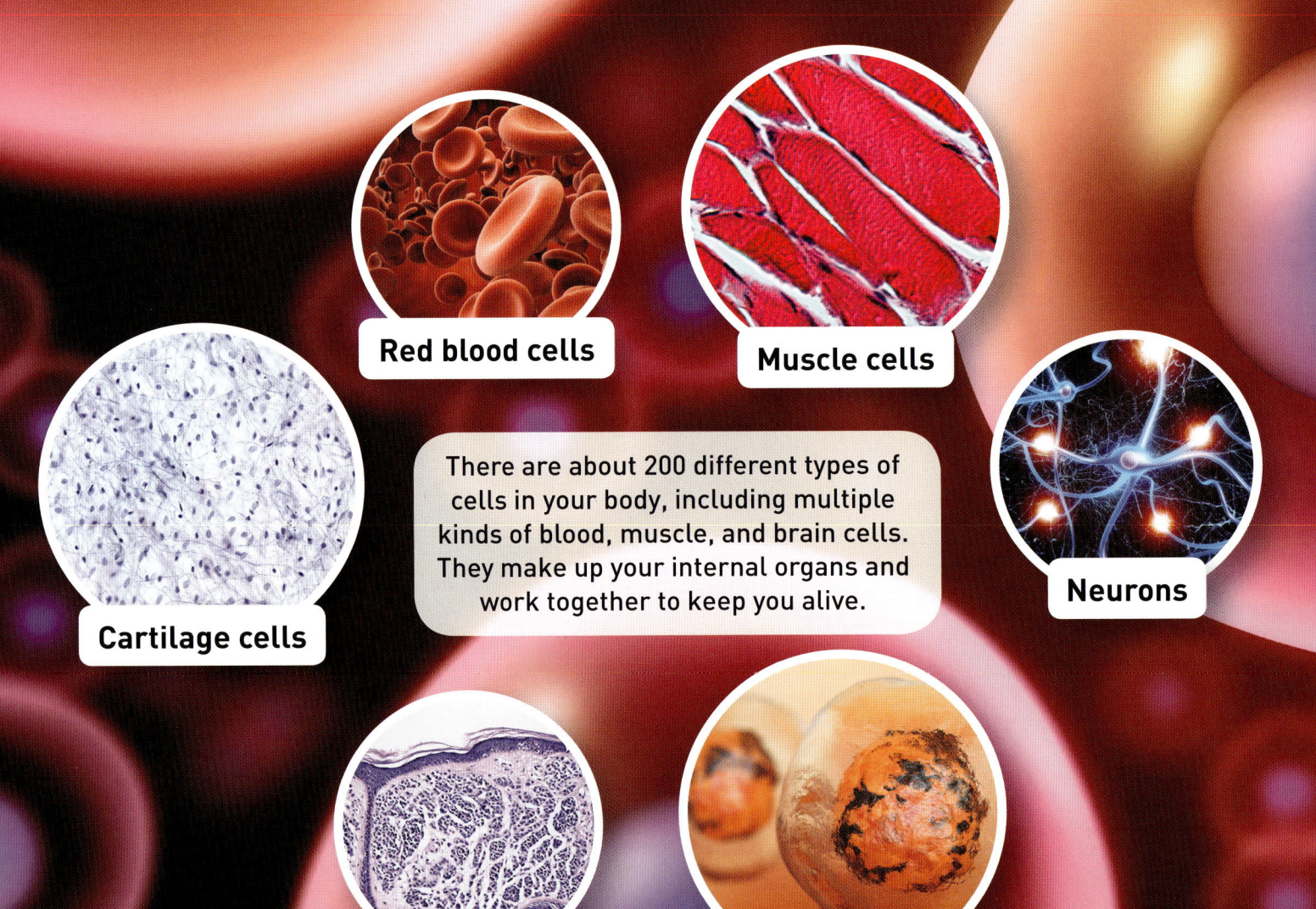

Red blood cells

Muscle cells

Cartilage cells

There are about 200 different types of cells in your body, including multiple kinds of blood, muscle, and brain cells. They make up your internal organs and work together to keep you alive.

Neurons

Skin cells

Stem cells

You have about **100 trillion** (100,000,000,000,000) cells in your body.

Most of your cells have a **24-hour life cycle** before they split and become two separate cells.

Each day, up to **30 billion** of your cells die. For adults, up to 70 billion cells die each day. (Don't worry, they're replaced by new ones all the time.)

The largest cell in the human body is the **female egg cell**.

THE HUMAN BODY

Bones
YOUR AMAZING SKELETON

Inside your body are 206 bones. They give you shape and structure. They help you stand and help hold you together. Here are some awesome facts about your skeleton.

DID YOU KNOW?

When you are born, your body has about 300 bones. That's almost 100 more bones than in an adult skeleton. As you grow, many smaller bones fuse together to form some of the bigger parts of your skeleton.

UNCOMMON CENTER

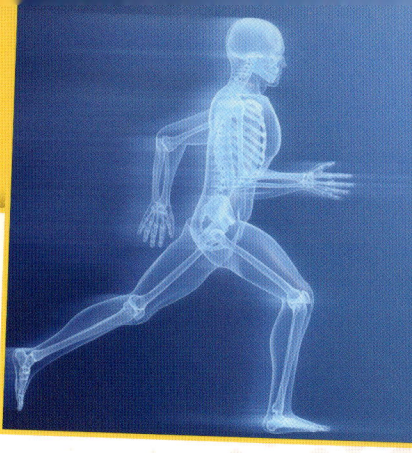

Humans are vertebrates, or animals with backbones. Less than 10 percent of living animal species are vertebrates.

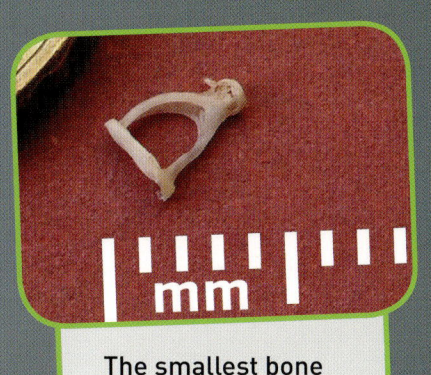

The smallest bone in your body is inside your ear. The stirrup-shaped **stapes bone** measures about 0.08 to 0.1 inches (2 to 3 millimeters) across.

The largest bone in your body is the **femur**, the bone that runs from your hip to your knee.

More than half your body's bones are in your **hands** and **feet**.

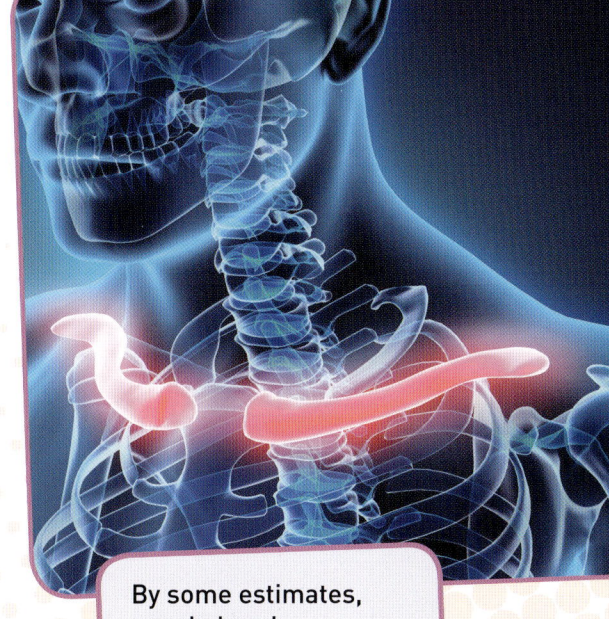

By some estimates, people break **collarbones** more often than any other bone.

THE HUMAN BODY

Drop by Drop

FACTS ABOUT BLOOD

Your heart pumps blood through your body, sending each blood cell on a trip that lasts about a minute. Blood lets your body breathe by carrying oxygen from your lungs to all of your organs. Here are some amazing facts about the precious liquid.

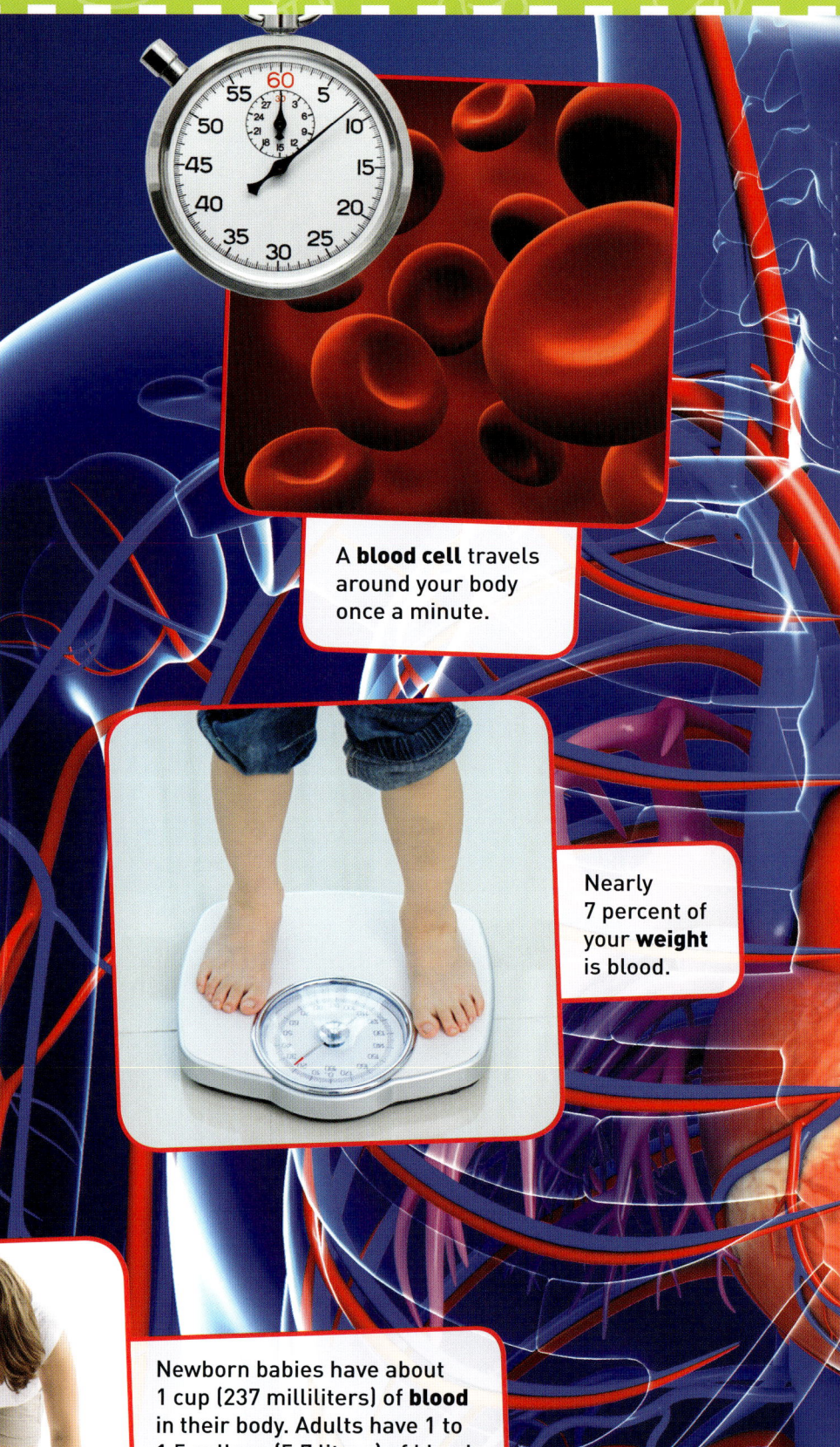

A **blood cell** travels around your body once a minute.

Nearly 7 percent of your **weight** is blood.

Newborn babies have about 1 cup (237 milliliters) of **blood** in their body. Adults have 1 to 1.5 gallons (5.7 liters) of blood in their bodies.

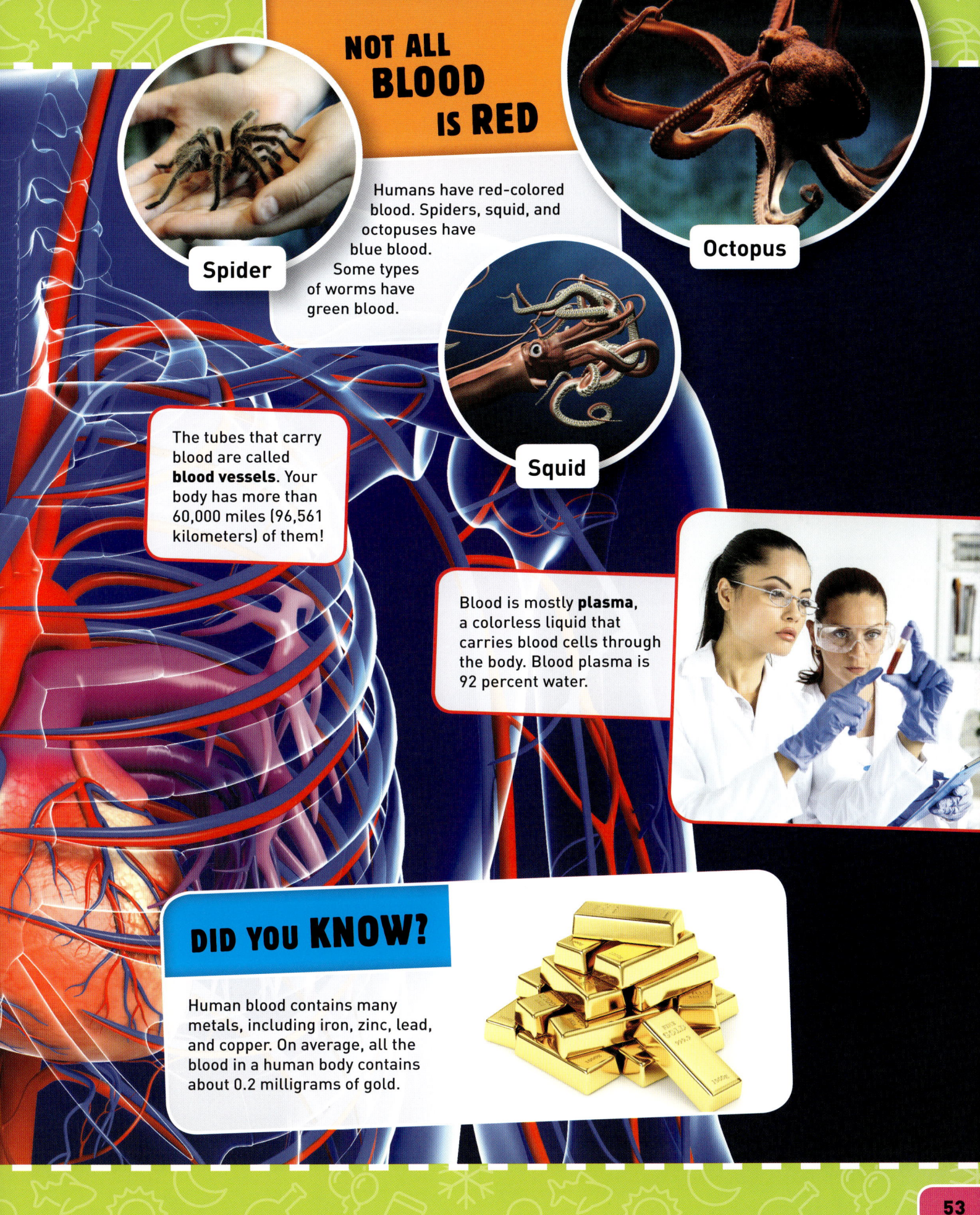

NOT ALL BLOOD IS RED

Spider

Octopus

Humans have red-colored blood. Spiders, squid, and octopuses have blue blood. Some types of worms have green blood.

Squid

The tubes that carry blood are called **blood vessels**. Your body has more than 60,000 miles (96,561 kilometers) of them!

Blood is mostly **plasma**, a colorless liquid that carries blood cells through the body. Blood plasma is 92 percent water.

DID YOU KNOW?

Human blood contains many metals, including iron, zinc, lead, and copper. On average, all the blood in a human body contains about 0.2 milligrams of gold.

THE HUMAN BODY

Skin makes up about 15 percent of your body weight.

Skin is the largest **organ** of the human body. On average, a human's skin is about 19 square feet (1.8 square meters).

28 DAYS LATER

Your body sheds dead skin cells all the time. Every hour, you lose about 30,000 dead cells. You grow a new layer of skin every 28 days.

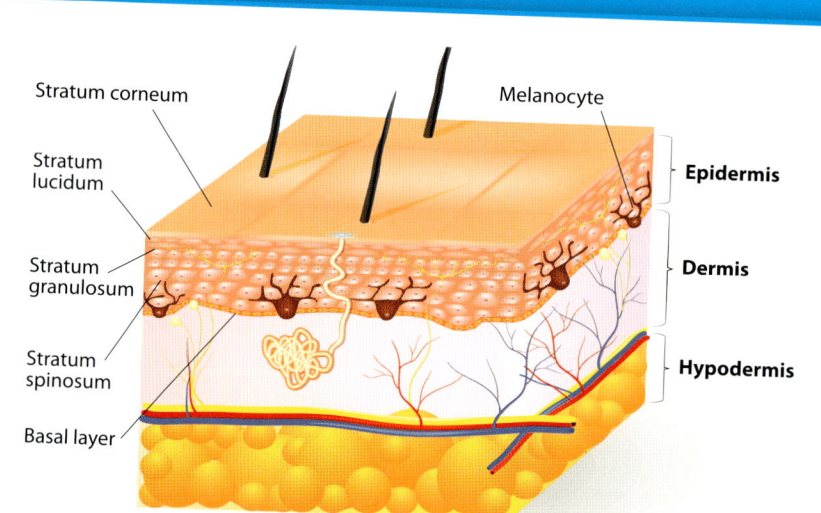

The Outside Story

FACTS ABOUT YOUR SKIN

Skin protects your body from the world outside. It blocks dirt, germs, radiation, and a lot of other harmful things from getting at your organs. It can even repair itself. Here are some amazing facts about human "armor."

Your skin varies in thickness all over your body. Your thinnest skin is on your **eyelids**, where it is just 0.002 inches (0.05 millimeters) thick.

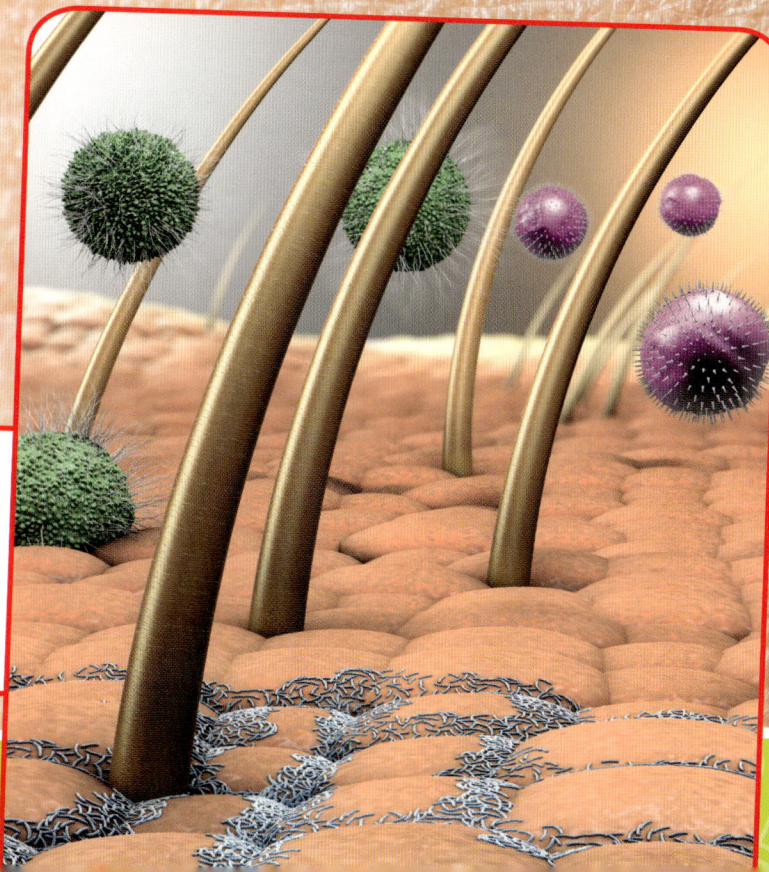

Your skin is home to about 1,000 different species of **bacteria**.

THE HUMAN BODY

Hair and Now

FACTS ABOUT YOUR HAIR

On average, the **life span** of any individual hair is two to seven years.

Each year, you **grow** about 6 inches (154 millimeters) of hair.

You **lose** around 50 to 100 hairs each day.

The **world record** for the longest hair is held by a woman whose hair measured 18.4 feet (5.6 meters). It took more than 30 years to grow it that long.

RARELY RED

- Black hair is the most common hair color.
- Only 2 percent of the world's population has naturally blond hair.
- Less than 2 percent of the world's population has naturally red-colored hair.

If a man never shaved, his **beard** would grow about 30 feet (9 meters) in his lifetime.

On average, people have 100,000 **hair follicles** (the part of the skin where hair grows) on their heads.

A **single hair** is strong enough to hold 3.5 ounces (100 grams) before breaking.

THE HUMAN BODY

Brains!

THE ORGAN THAT REALLY MAKES YOU THINK

DID YOU KNOW?

Your brain is always working, even when you're sleeping. It keeps busy, running your body's systems and generating dreams. In fact, during some stages of sleep, your brain is as active as when you are awake.

Your brain is a cantaloupe-sized, grayish-pink blob with the consistency of gelatin. That may not sound very special—but it is! Your brain controls your body and thoughts. Read these facts so your brain can learn them!

Your **brain** is almost 75 percent water.

It's been estimated that your brain has **50,000 to 70,000 thoughts** each day.

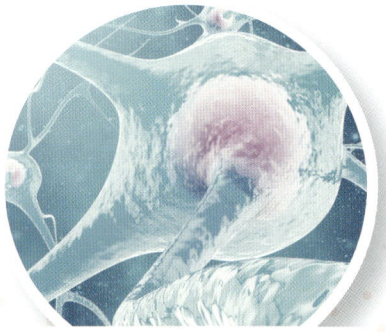

Nerve signals travel to and from the brain at speeds of up to 270 miles (435 kilometers) per hour.

About 20 percent of your body's **oxygen** goes to your brain.

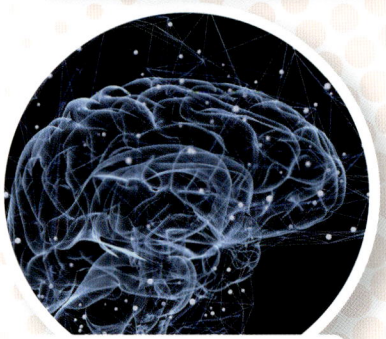

When you are awake, your brain can use as much **energy** as a light bulb.

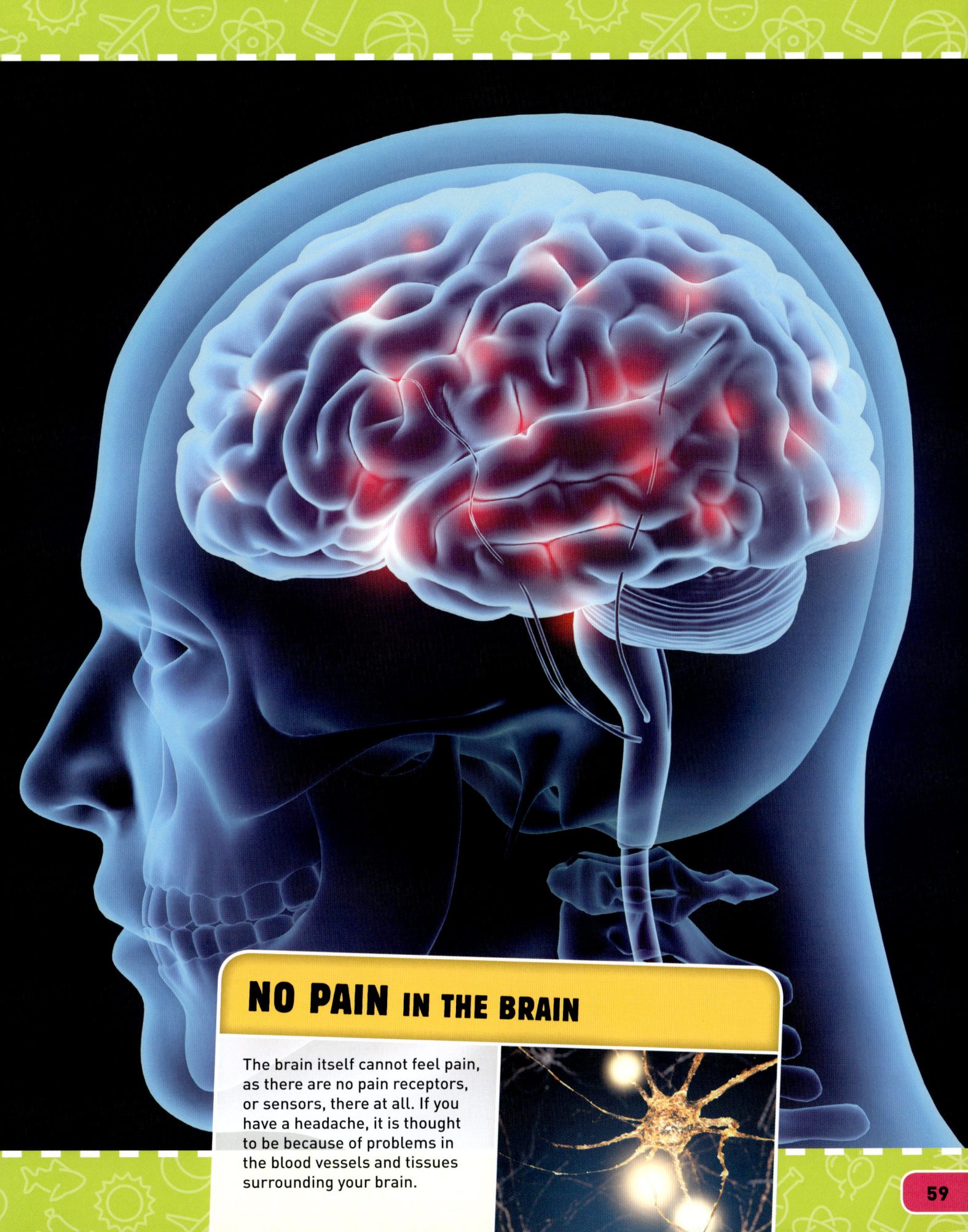

NO PAIN IN THE BRAIN

The brain itself cannot feel pain, as there are no pain receptors, or sensors, there at all. If you have a headache, it is thought to be because of problems in the blood vessels and tissues surrounding your brain.

THE HUMAN BODY

Wild Comparisons

HUMANS VS ANIMALS

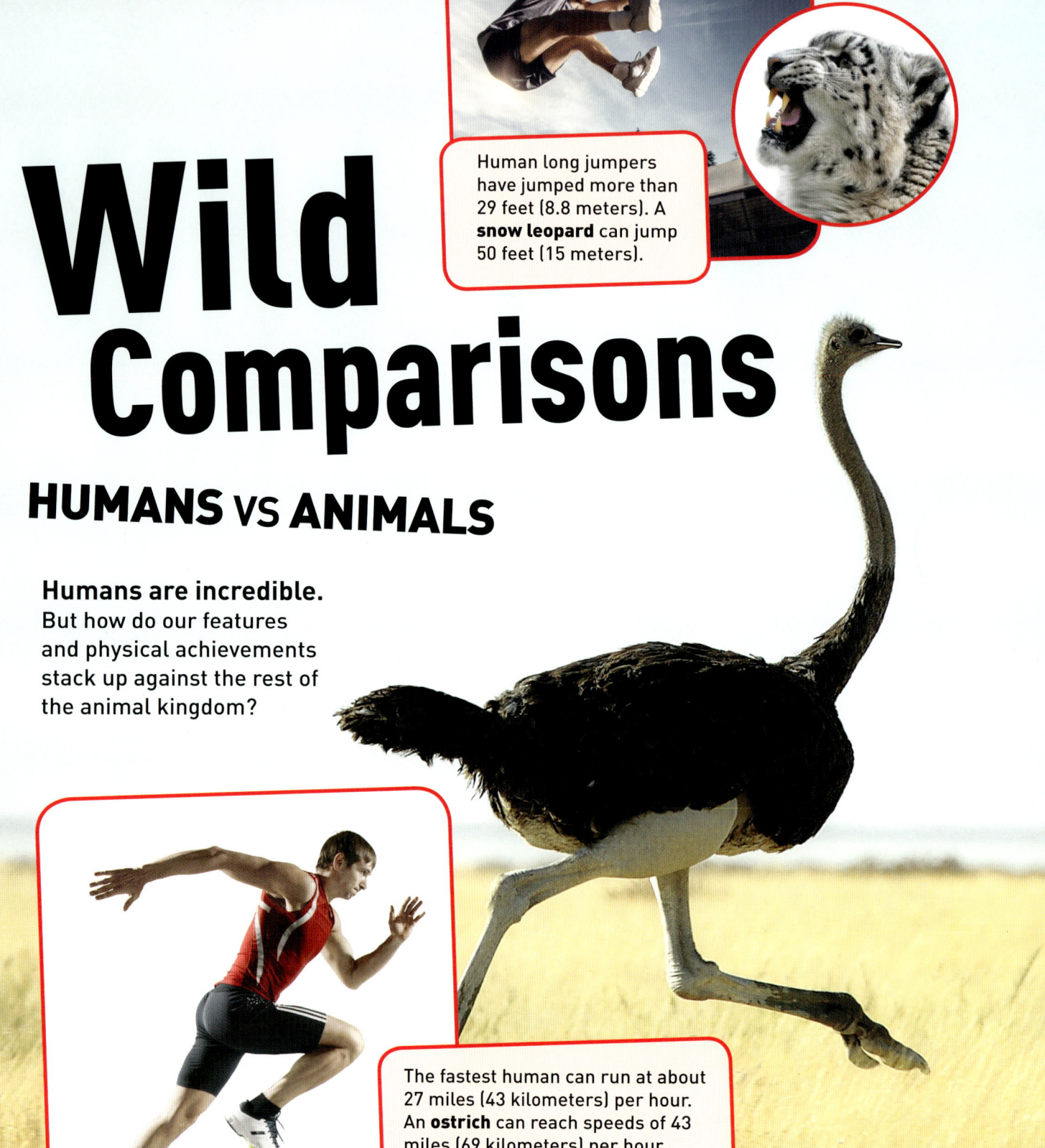

Human long jumpers have jumped more than 29 feet (8.8 meters). A **snow leopard** can jump 50 feet (15 meters).

Humans are incredible. But how do our features and physical achievements stack up against the rest of the animal kingdom?

The fastest human can run at about 27 miles (43 kilometers) per hour. An **ostrich** can reach speeds of 43 miles (69 kilometers) per hour.

A human weight lifter might lift about 586 pounds (266 kilograms). An **elephant** can lift more than 661 pounds (300 kilograms) with its trunk.

A human free diver can dive more than 400 feet (122 meters) below the ocean's surface. Some **whales** can dive to 10,000 feet (3,048 meters).

A human swimming champ can swim over 5 miles (8 kilometers) per hour. **Tunas** can cruise at over 43 miles (70 kilometers) per hour.

SCIENCE AND TECHNOLOGY

600 BCE
A Greek scientist named Thales of Miletus discovers the hair-raising principle of static electricity.

725 CE
Tick tock! The first mechanical clock is made by a Chinese Buddhist monk named Yi Xing.

1206
Turkish scholar and inventor Ismail al-Jazari completes his book on engineering. It describes 50 different machines, including a drink-serving automaton.

1593
One of the greatest astronomers of all time, Galileo Galilei, invents an early form of the thermometer.

600 BCE — 400 BCE — 200 BCE — 1 CE — 200 — 400 — 600 — 800 — 1000 — 1200 — 1400 — 1600

1665
Thanks to a deadly plague that sends him home from his university, Sir Isaac Newton has the chance to start developing the laws of gravity as we know them today.

1800
In Italy, Alessandro Volta creates the first battery.

1895
Wilhelm Röntgen discovers X-rays.

1888
Nikola Tesla patents the AC induction motor. (These motors run most of your household appliances.)

1660 — 1680 — 1700 — 1720 — 1740 — 1760 — 1780 — 1800 — 1820 — 1840 — 1860 — 1880 — 1900

Discover the Past

TIME TRAVEL THROUGH SCIENCE AND TECHNOLOGY HISTORY

Some serious brainpower led to these great discoveries and inventions.

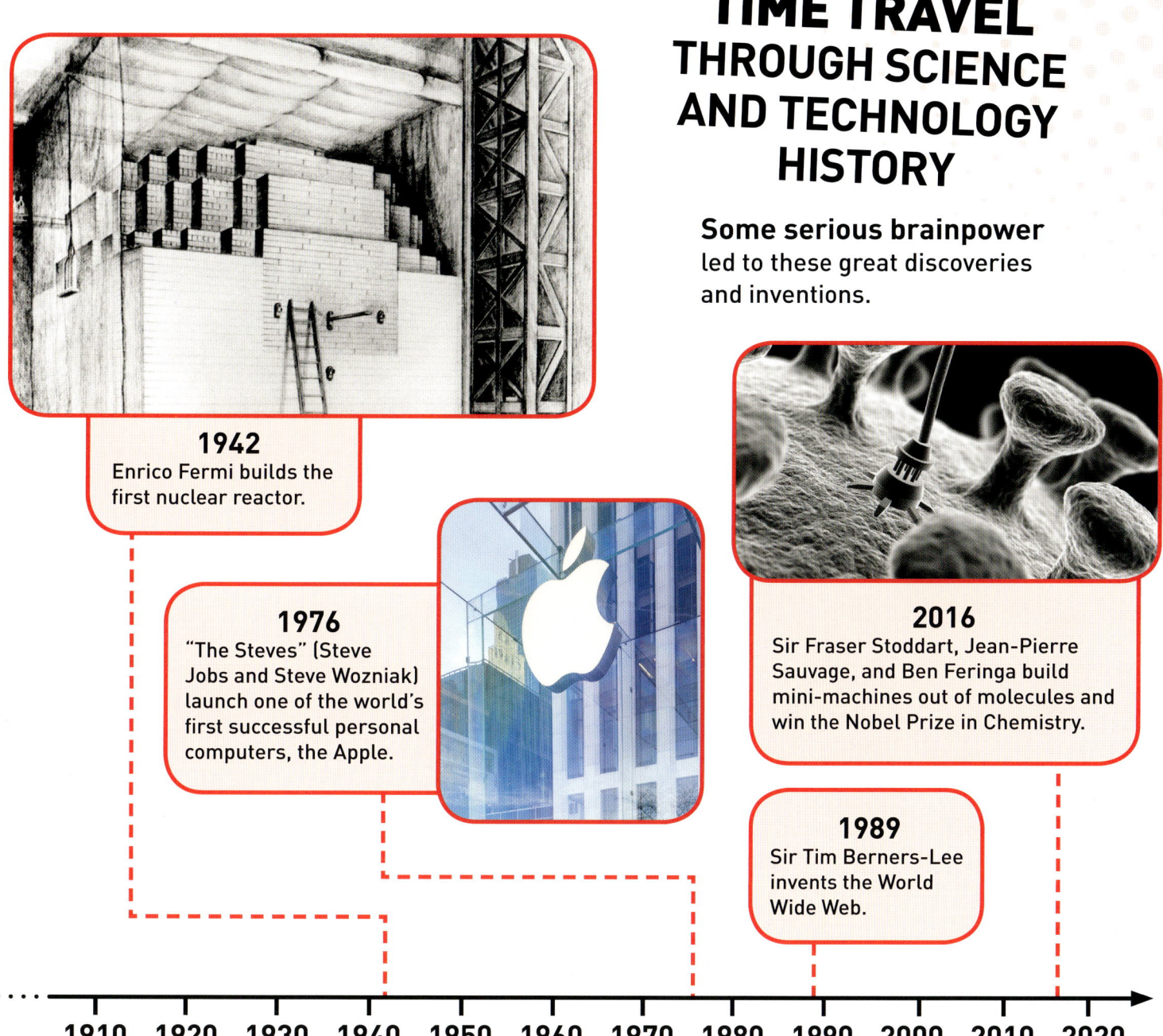

1942
Enrico Fermi builds the first nuclear reactor.

1976
"The Steves" (Steve Jobs and Steve Wozniak) launch one of the world's first successful personal computers, the Apple.

2016
Sir Fraser Stoddart, Jean-Pierre Sauvage, and Ben Feringa build mini-machines out of molecules and win the Nobel Prize in Chemistry.

1989
Sir Tim Berners-Lee invents the World Wide Web.

SCIENCE AND TECHNOLOGY

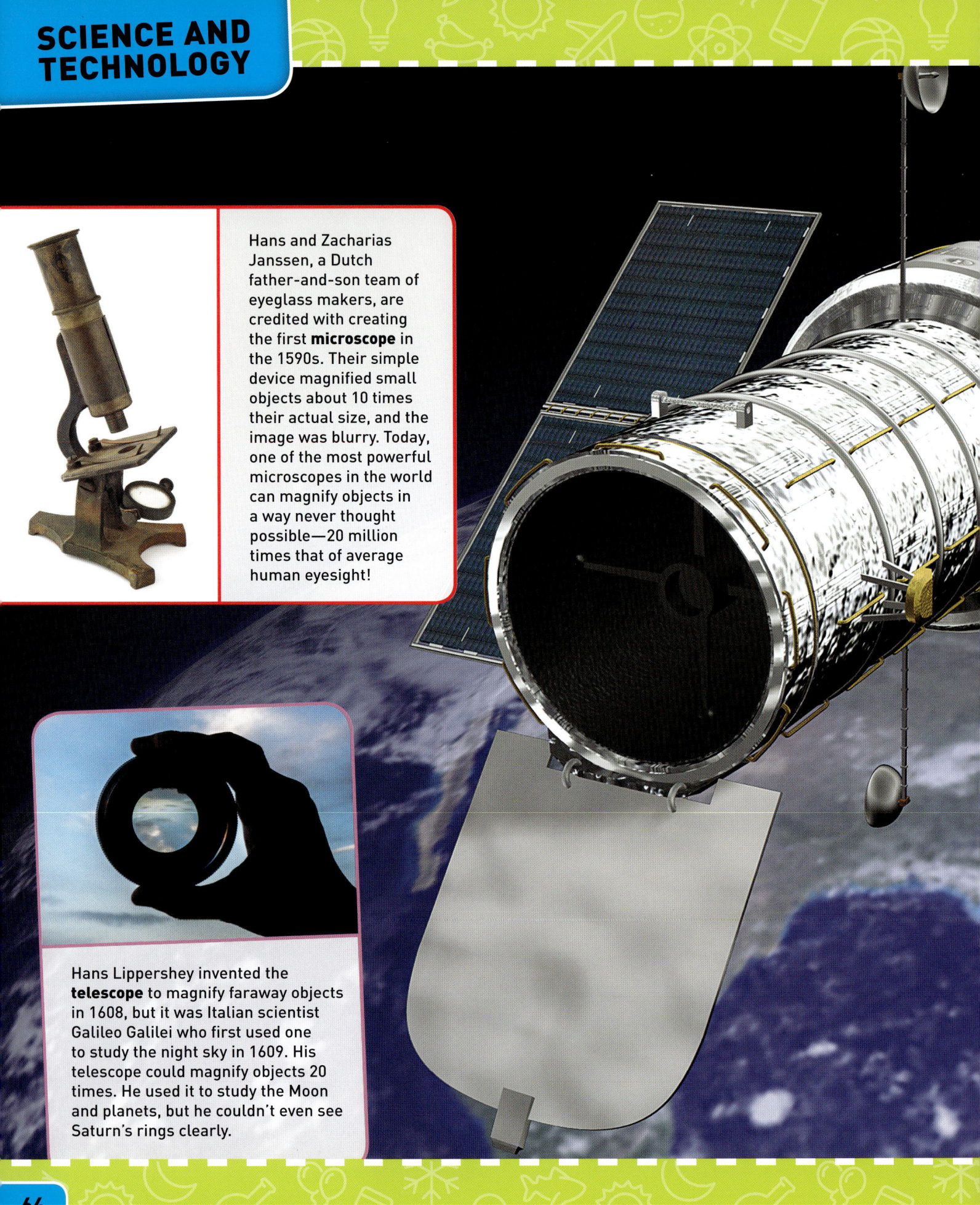

Hans and Zacharias Janssen, a Dutch father-and-son team of eyeglass makers, are credited with creating the first **microscope** in the 1590s. Their simple device magnified small objects about 10 times their actual size, and the image was blurry. Today, one of the most powerful microscopes in the world can magnify objects in a way never thought possible—20 million times that of average human eyesight!

Hans Lippershey invented the **telescope** to magnify faraway objects in 1608, but it was Italian scientist Galileo Galilei who first used one to study the night sky in 1609. His telescope could magnify objects 20 times. He used it to study the Moon and planets, but he couldn't even see Saturn's rings clearly.

Viewfinder

SEE A NEW WORLD THROUGH A LENS

Telescopes and microscopes give us a clear look at things impossible to see with the human eye alone.

DID YOU KNOW?

- Electron microscopes use beams of electrons—the tiny, negatively charged particles found in atoms—to magnify objects up to two million times their actual size.
- Some telescopes can detect a form of extreme radiation known as gamma rays. Gamma-ray telescopes can be used to find radiation from massive explosions throughout the universe.
- The James Webb Space Telescope will be the largest and most powerful telescope launched into space. Its mission is to find information about how galaxies are formed.

FUN FACTS!

- The first microscopes were called "flea glasses" because they were used to study insects.
- Microscopes changed the practice of medicine. Before them, people believed poisonous gases or evil spirits caused illness. Using microscopes, scientists could see viruses and bacteria, the real causes of illness.
- As big as a school bus and weighing more than 24,500 pounds (11,110 kilograms), the Hubble Space Telescope is the most productive scientific instrument ever built.

SCIENCE AND TECHNOLOGY

In the first century CE, Hero, an engineer from Alexandria, Egypt, invented an early **steam-driven turbine**. Nearly 2,000 years later, steam turbines are still one of the most common ways to generate electric power. Many factories and power plants rely on steam power.

Fire is a tool. Archaeologists explored a cave in South Africa where humans (and our ancestors) had been living for two million years. They found the remains of campfires that were lit 1.2 million years ago!

Tools help to keep us alive. In 1982, Barney Clark, a retired dentist, was the first person to receive an artificial heart designed for permanent use. Today, scientists have been using **3D printers** to create ears, bones, and organs, such as kidneys. One day, your doctor may be able to print the body part you need!

ANIMALS USE TOOLS, TOO!

- Chimps make tools to dig for ants and even spears for hunting.
- Dolphins use sea sponges to protect their noses while uncovering prey on the seafloor.
- Sea otters crack hard shells with rocks.
- Gorillas use branches and shrub trunks for walking sticks and bridges.

A team of experts named the **knife** as the number one tool in history. Knives help humans to hunt and cut up prey, build homes, and defend themselves.

When the Iron Age began, around 1200 BCE in Europe and the Middle East, **iron tools** spread quickly. Iron farming tools helped farmers plow tough soil. Iron weapons and armor helped armies win battles.

Open up nearly any electronic device, and you'll probably find a **transistor**. Developed in 1947 at Bell Laboratories, they control the electric current that flows through a circuit. You wouldn't be able to watch TV or talk on your cell phone without them.

In the Toolbox

TOOLS MAKE OUR LIVES EASIER

For the ancestors of modern humans, the first tools were rocks, which were used to bang, smash, and carve things more than three million years ago. Can you imagine what they would think if they could see a mobile phone? Yes, your phone is a tool. A tool is anything that helps you get a job or task done. Think of the next thing you have to do. Will you use any tools to help you?

SCIENCE AND TECHNOLOGY

History's Mysteries

SOME ANCIENT WORKS REMAIN A PUZZLE

Monuments and artifacts from long ago help us to piece together our understanding of the past. Yet there are many places and things whose stories we don't fully know.

The white lines in the red and tan desert of southern Peru might not look like anything special when you're on the ground. But from high above, you can see that the **Nazca lines** are actually pictures scratched into the landscape. These pictures are called geoglyphs, and the ancient Nazca made more than a thousand of them! Unfortunately, they left no records to tell us why.

THE ANTIKYTHERA MECHANISM

Back in 1901, pieces of a 2,000-year-old device were fished out of the Mediterranean Sea. Scientists think it may have been a planetary clock. However, similar technology does not appear again until over 1,000 years after this device was made.

THE UFFINGTON WHITE HORSE

Up on a hill near Uffington, England, chalk-filled trenches create the shape of a huge white horse. It might be more than 3,000 years old. No one knows who made it or why.

THE HYPOGEUM OF HAL SAFLIENI

More than 5,000 years old, the limestone Hypogeum in Malta is possibly the oldest underground temple in the world. Inside is the mysterious Oracle Chamber, where even the tiniest whisper can be heard from clear across the room. How and why remain unknown.

SCIENCE AND TECHNOLOGY

Perfect for lovers of science fiction, the **Futuro** was a prefabricated home kit designed in 1968.

If you don't like noisy neighbors, this **house on a rock** in Serbia is the place to be.

Do you hate staying in one place? The **Walking House** can get you wherever you want to go.

Home Sweet Home

EVERYONE NEEDS A PLACE TO LIVE IN, BUT THESE HOMES ARE **REALLY EXCEPTIONAL!**

An **upside-down home**, like this one in Germany, could turn your whole world around!

This tiny, teapot-shaped house was actually a **gas station,** built in 1922 in Zillah, Washington.

SCIENCE AND TECHNOLOGY

Going Up

SKYSCRAPERS REACH FOR THE SKY

For centuries, builders and architects have thrown up taller and taller constructions. Will they ever stop? As long as engineering skills and new materials are developed, the answer is . . . nope!

At 2,717 feet (828 meters) tall, the **Burj Khalifa** in Dubai, UAE, is the reigning champ of tall towers. But don't worry, taller buildings are already in the works.

THE EMPIRE STATE BUILDING UNITED STATES

At 1,454 feet (443 meters) tall, the Empire State Building in New York City was the world's tallest from 1931 to 1972. It is still one of the most famous and recognizable of all buildings.

PYRAMID OF CHEOPS, EGYPT

This Great Pyramid in Giza, Egypt was built around 2500 BCE. Originally 481 feet (147 meters) tall, it was the tallest man-made construction for over 3,800 years.

ULM MINSTER, GERMANY

At 530 feet (162 meters) tall, this church in Ulm, Germany, is the tallest church in the world.

THE EIFFEL TOWER, FRANCE

At 1,063 feet (324 meters) tall, Paris' famous tower was the tallest construction in the world from 1889 to 1930.

MET LIFE TOWER, UNITED STATES

Built in 1909, the Met Life Tower in New York City was the first building to reach a height of 700 feet (213 meters). But it was the world's tallest for only four years.

SCIENCE AND TECHNOLOGY

THE PALM JUMEIRAH, UNITED ARAB EMIRATES

Built off the coast of Dubai, this artificial archipelago, or island group, is shaped like a palm tree. Supporting hundreds of homes and dozens of hotels and businesses, the construction has added 320 miles (515 kilometers) to Dubai's coastline.

The **Sydney Opera House**, a complex of performance spaces, is the jewel of Sydney Harbour, Australia.

Wow in the World!

AMAZING CONSTRUCTIONS CATCH YOUR EYE.

Beyond tall structures and skyscraping office towers, some of the world's greatest constructions have been built to make us marvel at the designer's imagination.

THE APPLE "MOTHERSHIP," CALIFORNIA

Apple Inc.'s new headquarters in California is a giant, ring-shaped building that can hold more than 12,000 employees.

SAGRADA FAMÍLIA, SPAIN

This amazing church in Barcelona has been in the works for 135 years. Still under construction, it's clearly like no other church in the world.

SCIENCE AND TECHNOLOGY

The road-building techniques of the ancient **Roman Empire** have stood the test of time. Some are still in use after 2,000 years of traffic!

In the early 1800s, John McAdam, a Scottish engineer, developed a process to **pave** roads. It involved packing down layers of soil and crushed stones in a roadbed. Later, people improved on his method by adding tar to bind the soil and rocks.

On the Road

THEY DIG, DUMP, AND PAVE A PATH FOR YOU

Life is a highway when you're working in the world of heavy equipment.

If you want to move around dirt and other things with your very own **bulldozer**, you had better have a lot of money in your piggy bank. Prices begin at around $30,000 and range up to $200,000 or more. The most commonly purchased models (with 110 to 130 horsepower) usually cost $75,000 to $175,000.

Meet the **Bagger 293**, the largest-ever land vehicle. This super-sized excavator can move 8.5 million cubic feet (240,700 cubic meters) of dirt a day.

A **dragline excavator** is used to raise and lower buckets of soil and rocks. Most draglines weigh around 8,000 tons (7,257 metric tons)—that's about the weight of 40 blue whales, the largest animal known to have ever lived on the planet.

FUN FACTS!

- The longest interstate highway that stretches across the continental U.S. is I-90. It takes a little more than 3,000 miles (4,828 kilometers) to get from Seattle, Washington, to Boston, Massachusetts, on that road.
- All in all, the U.S. Interstate Highway System is more than 46,000 miles (74,030 kilometers) long.
- I-95 travels through 15 states, from Maine to Florida.
- The Pan-American Highway connects almost every country in North and South America. There's just one gap of about 60 miles (97 kilometers).

Brothers Chester and Charles Foote developed the first **concrete paving rig** by putting together a concrete mixer and a distribution machine. Later, the Foote Company added an engine and crawlers, or tracks, instead of wheels.

SCIENCE AND TECHNOLOGY

How Low Can You Go?
FOUR OF THE DEEPEST HOLES EVER DUG BY HUMANS

Over the years, miners, explorers, and scientists have shoveled, blasted, and drilled into the depths of the Earth in search of oil, riches, or new discoveries. Here are some of the most awesome excavations.

Starting in 1871, nearly 50,000 miners used pickaxes and shovels to dig in the **Kimberley diamond mine** in South Africa. At more than 705 feet (215 meters) deep and 1,500 feet (457 meters) wide, it is one of the world's biggest handmade pits.

Dug more than 100 years ago, the **Bingham Canyon Mine** in Utah is one of the world's biggest copper mines. At 3,000 feet (914 meters) deep, this massive excavation is also the deepest open-pit mine.

The **Berkeley Pit copper mine** in Montana reached a depth of 1,700 feet (518 meters) before it was closed in 1982. Since then, it has filled up with more than 900 feet (274 meters) of water. Scientists work to keep birds away because the water has so many leftover heavy metals and chemicals in it.

The **Kola Superdeep Borehole** in Russia was an experiment to see how far down a hole could reach. The Russians drilled from 1970 to 1992, reaching a depth of more than 40,000 feet (12,262 meters) before stopping. It ranks as the world's deepest hole.

JOURNEY TO THE CENTER OF THE EARTH?

Not even close! Earth's crust is a solid layer of rock that, under the continents, averages about 22 to 44 miles (35 to 70 kilometers) in thickness. Beneath that, the mantle is a layer of semi-solid materials that extends for about 1,800 miles (2,897 kilometers). Earth's core consists of a solid center surrounded by an outer layer of liquid.

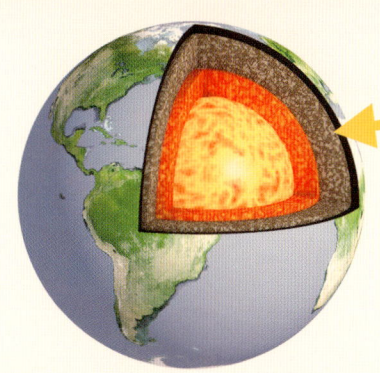

SCIENCE AND TECHNOLOGY

Incredible Crossings

AMAZING FEATS OF ENGINEERING!

Bridges help people get across road-blocking obstacles and waterways. They also can be some of the most beautiful examples of engineering in the world.

In August 2016, the **Zhangjiajie Grand Canyon Bridge**, the world's highest and longest glass-bottom bridge, was opened for visitors in China. It was temporarily closed after just a few days because too many people showed up to cross the bridge!

Does China's **Anji Bridge** remind you of anything? It has been compared to a rainbow because of its large central arch. It is also the oldest standing bridge in China.

The **Khaju Bridge** in Iran, built around 1650 CE, doesn't just help move people from one place to another; it regulates the flow of river water, too.

Pont du Gard Aqueduct in France was built by the Roman Empire between 19 BCE and 60 CE. The stones were cut to fit together perfectly—there is no mortar holding them together!

The world's longest suspension bridge is Japan's Akashi Kaikyō Bridge, or **Pearl Bridge.** It has a total length of 12,831 feet (3,911 meters) and a central span length—measured between the bridge's towers—of 6,532 feet (1,991 meters).

In Colorado, bridge jumpers flock to the **Royal Gorge Bridge** as part of a thrill-seeking sport. Standing 955 feet (291 meters) above the Arkansas River, it is the highest suspension bridge in the U.S.

SCIENCE AND TECHNOLOGY

If crowded trains are not your thing, you might look to the future. Some cities are looking into train systems that have individual pods. Ithaca, New York, and Greenville, South Carolina, have both proposed becoming the first **podcar** city in the U.S.

A **bullet train** is a high-speed passenger train that can travel more than 199 miles (320 kilometers) per hour. China built the largest bullet-train network in less than 10 years. Its 12,500 miles (20,117 kilometers) of rail lines is more than the rest of the world has combined.

Maglev trains have superconducting magnets instead of wheels. They glide just above the tracks at speeds up to 374 miles (603 kilometers) per hour—that's the record-breaking speed of one Japanese maglev train. It's more than twice as fast as the fastest trains in the U.S.

Aboard the **Trans-Siberian Railway**, you'll travel almost 6,152 miles (9,258 kilometers) and pass through two continents and eight time zones.

ALL ABOARD! Ride the Rails

Trains have been moving masses of people for almost 200 years.

The Tube, the nickname for London's subway system, was the world's first underground railway and has been transporting passengers since 1863. More than 1.3 billion passengers ride the city's metro system every year.

DID YOU KNOW?

- A horse beat the first American steam locomotive in a race.
- The world has standardized time zones because of train travel.
- The longest railway platform is at the Gorakhpur station in Uttar Pradesh, India. It is 4,483 feet (1,366 meters) long.

The world's first **locomotive** trip was a short journey, traveling 9 miles (14 kilometers) in South Wales on February 21, 1804. But Richard Trevithick's locomotive ran into difficulty on the way back. The boiler leaked, and the engine was too heavy for the rails.

SCIENCE AND TECHNOLOGY

Steering column **Driver's seat** **Engine**

Wheel **Chain**

The earliest cars, called **horseless carriages**, were powered by steam engines.

Electric cars have been around since the 1800s, but they were expensive and couldn't drive very far without a charge. Today, the electric car market is soaring, and there are more than 16,000 charging stations across the United States.

Automobile companies are always changing their ideas about the future of the car. A few have been working on car designs that run mostly on **solar power**. These cars collect energy from the Sun through solar roof panels.

There's debate over who invented the first gasoline-powered automobile, but there's no doubt Henry Ford's **Model T** brought affordable cars to Americans and transformed the transportation industry. Ford developed the moving assembly line mode of production in 1913. Where it once took 12 hours to build a car, with Ford's production methods, it took less than three.

Le Mans, sometimes called the Grand Prix of Endurance and Efficiency, is a 24-hour car race that has been held nearly every year since 1923 in Le Mans, France. Since 1928, the race's winner is whichever team of drivers has gotten the farthest by the end of the day.

In the Driver's Seat
REV YOUR ENGINES . . .

Cars have given people the freedom to travel long distances at faster speeds, and people really seem to enjoy that freedom. There are more than a billion cars on the world's roads!

SCIENCE AND TECHNOLOGY

Today, the skies over the United States are home to around 5,000 commercial planes at any given time. The largest passenger plane is the **Airbus A380**, which can carry more than 850 passengers in its double-deck cabin. It is also one of the quietest wide-body jets currently in the sky.

Early models of **flying cars** have taken test flights, but the aircraft are still in the planning and development stage. The future may hold a traffic-filled sky!

Charles Lindbergh took off in the *Spirit of St. Louis* from New York on May 20, 1927, determined to become the first solo pilot to cross the Atlantic Ocean. He landed 33.5 hours later in Paris, France, welcomed by a crowd of thousands that had gathered to celebrate his success.

In 1849, a 10-year-old boy took a short flight in one of Sir George Cayley's **gliding machines**. Cayley's work designing, building, and testing flying machines inspired the first airplanes.

Failure didn't stop Wilbur and Orville Wright. Their first **Wright Flyer**, an engine-powered glider, lifted off the ground on December 17, 1903, but only stayed up for 12 seconds on the first flight. It was difficult to control, and it was damaged beyond repair when a gust of wind knocked it over. Almost two years later, though, on October 5, 1905, Wilbur piloted their new model, the *Flyer III*, until it ran out of gas after nearly 40 minutes of flight.

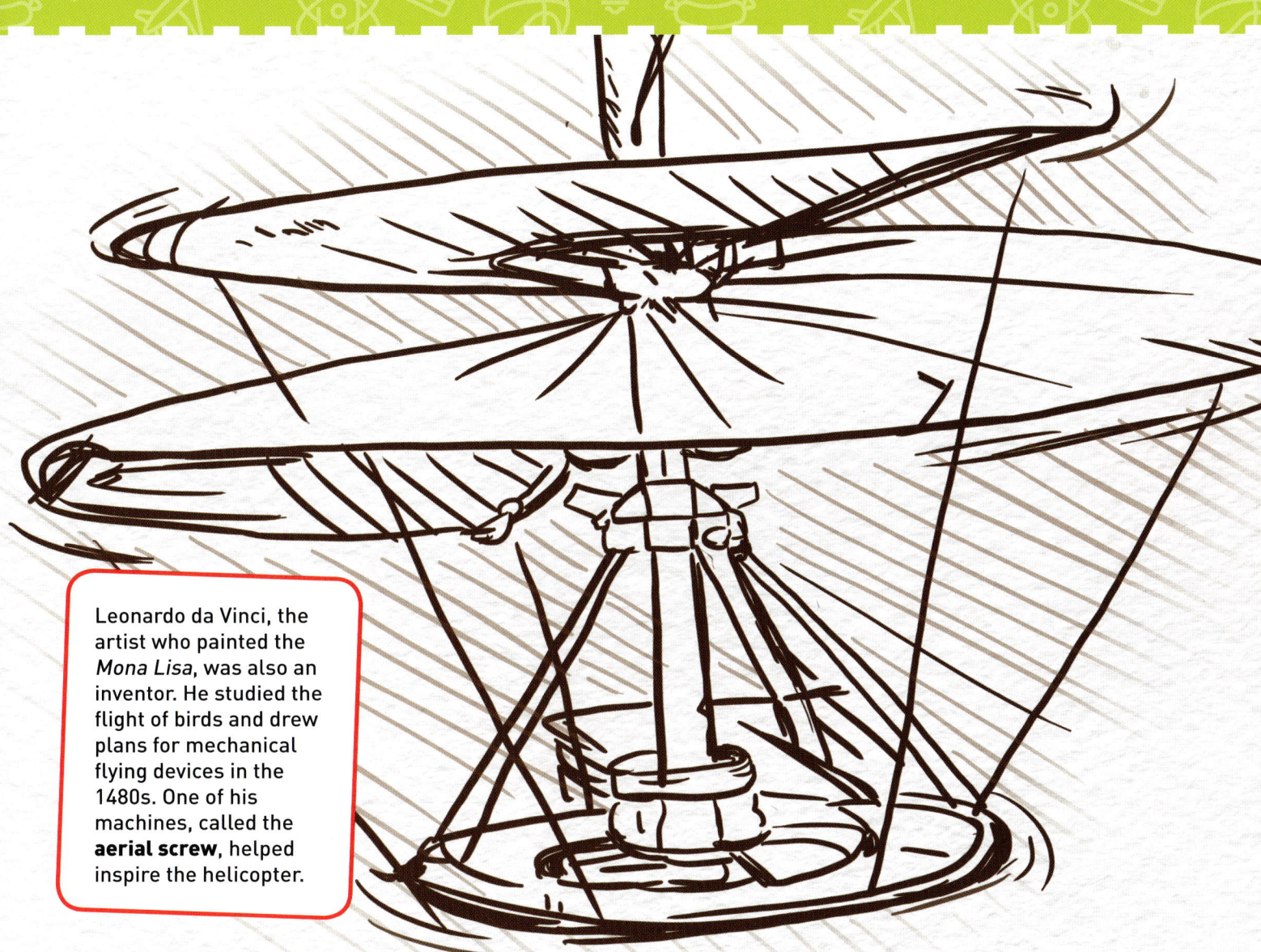

Leonardo da Vinci, the artist who painted the *Mona Lisa*, was also an inventor. He studied the flight of birds and drew plans for mechanical flying devices in the 1480s. One of his machines, called the **aerial screw**, helped inspire the helicopter.

High Flyers

PLANES AND HELICOPTERS TRANSFORMED TRAVEL AROUND THE WORLD

Humans tried to fly like birds for centuries. They were finally able to lift off the ground in hot-air balloons in the late 1700s, but it took more than another hundred years before the first airplane took flight.

SCIENCE AND TECHNOLOGY

AROUND THE WORLD

On May 6, 1937, the German dirigible **Hindenburg** caught fire and crashed. Thirty-six people were killed. The age of luxury airship travel came to an abrupt end.

In 2002, Steve Fossett became the first person to fly solo around the world in the *Spirit of Freedom* balloon.

Balloons carry **sensors** to the edge of the atmosphere, collecting data for weather agencies and many other scientists.

FIRST IN FLIGHT

In 1783 in France, the Montgolfier brothers demonstrated the first trip by hot-air balloon. Their flight covered 1.2 miles (1.9 kilometers) in 10 minutes.

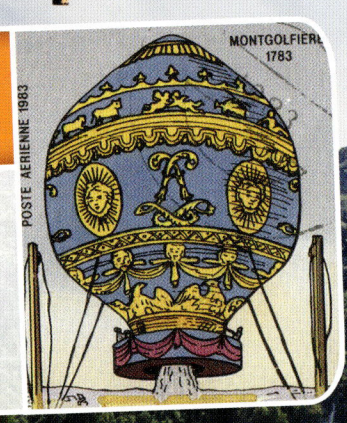

With the ability to stay aloft with heavy loads, many modern **blimps** are in development today.

Up, Up, and Away

BALLOONS AND AIRSHIPS TAKE TO THE SKY

Filled with hot air or helium, lighter-than-air vehicles carry passengers, cargo, and experiments high above the ground.

AIRSHIP? BLIMP? DIRIGIBLE?

An airship and a dirigible are the same thing. They are names for any vehicle that is inflated with a gas lighter than air, is powered, and can be steered. A rigid airship has a frame that gives it shape regardless of the gas inside. A blimp is an airship with no frame; if a blimp deflates, it loses its shape.

SCIENCE AND TECHNOLOGY

Survival Suits

AWESOME OUTFITS FOR EXTREME ENVIRONMENTS

Space suits like the **Extravehicular Mobility Unit (EMU)** provide a self-contained atmosphere, allowing astronauts to perform missions outside spacecraft.

From the depths of the sea to the vacuum of space, humans work and explore. Here are a few of the outfits that protect people in some of the hottest, coldest, and most dangerous places.

The lightweight armor of a **bomb suit** protects soldiers and other bomb technicians during bomb-defusing missions.

Cold-water and **ice rescue suits** provide protection by keeping out cold air and icy water during rescue missions.

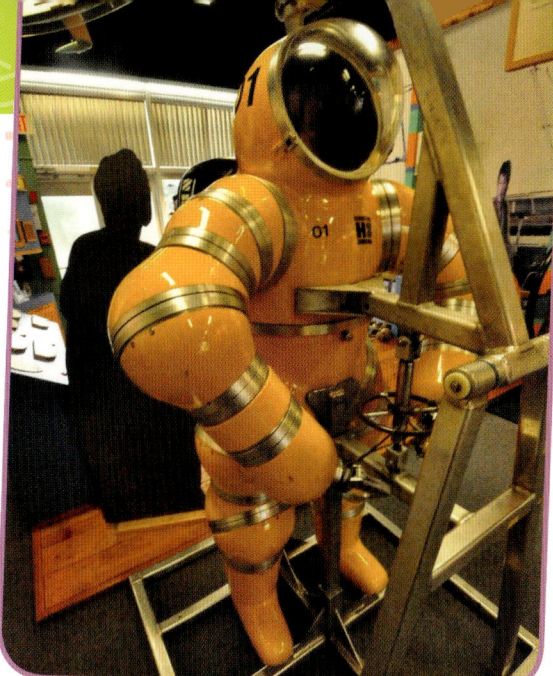

The hard-shelled **Exosuit Atmospheric Diving System** helps divers withstand extreme pressures up to 1,000 feet (305 meters) beneath the surface of the ocean.

The simple design of a **beekeeper suit** protects against thousands of bee stings.

A **Fire Proximity Suit** protects firefighters and volcano explorers from temperatures of up to 2,000 degrees Fahrenheit (1,093 degrees Celsius).

SCIENCE AND TECHNOLOGY

Processing Power

COMPUTERS ARE EVERYWHERE

Computers began as big, clunky machines that solved math problems. Today, they are household items that help us learn, play, shop, communicate, and manage nearly every part of our lives.

More and more, computers are built into everyday objects and connect to the Internet without screens or keyboards. In the future, we may live surrounded by computers without seeing any signs of them at all.

1820s

In the 1820s, Charles Babbage designed an early calculating machine called the Difference Engine. Never finished, the invention laid the groundwork for computers to come.

1946

Built in 1946, the first general-purpose programmable electronic digital computer was the Electronic Numerical Integrator and Computer (ENIAC). It weighed more than 30 tons (27 metric tons), and the U-shaped machine filled a 1,500-square-foot (139-square-meter) room.

1974

Considered by many to be the first personal computer, the Altair 8800 was created in 1974. They came as kits and had to be assembled.

DID YOU KNOW?

People normally blink about 17 times a minute. But while you stare at a screen, you blink only about seven times a minute!

1981

In 1981, the first commercially successful portable computer weighed more than 23 pounds (10 kilograms)!

1994

The first wearable mobile devices—digital watches and calculators—were introduced in the 1970s, but it wasn't until 1994 that the first device that combined computing and wireless communication went on sale.

SCIENCE AND TECHNOLOGY

CALLING ALL GERMS

One study has shown that mobile phones have 18 times more bacteria on them than toilet handles.

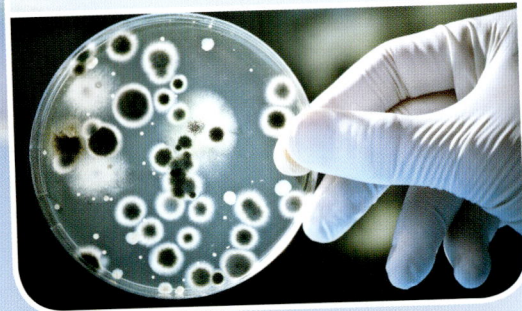

Today, about five billion people own mobile phones.

The first mobile phone call was made in 1973.

Phone Fever

AWESOME FACTS ABOUT MOBILE PHONES

Today, we use our mobile phones to talk, text, and send messages. We send pictures and communicate with live videos. Here are some amazing facts about our portable communicators.

Throwing mobile phones is a sport in Finland.

Around the world, more people have access to mobile phones than to toilets.

PHONE FEAR

A "nomophobic" person feels anxious when he or she doesn't have a mobile phone. "Nomo" is short for "no mobile."

SCIENCE AND TECHNOLOGY

Here Come the Robots

MACHINES OF TODAY AND TOMORROW

The first robot was invented more than 2,000 years ago by the ancient Greek mathematician Archytas. It was a steam-powered wooden pigeon that could fly. In 1921, Czech playwright Karel Čapek was the first person to use the word "robot." In a play, he wrote about human-like robots—before any such robots existed. Čapek didn't know his science-fiction fantasy would become a reality in our world.

The first **industrial robot** was a part of the General Motors automotive assembly line in 1961. More than a million robots work in factories today, and the number continues to grow.

It will probably be a long time before humans can visit Mars. However, robots—such as **NASA's *Opportunity***—have been exploring the surface of the Red Planet for years.

Many robots are run by remote control or follow preset instructions. **Artificial intelligence** gives robots the ability to learn, to make decisions on their own, and to even understand human emotions.

Firefighters are beginning to use **firefighting robots** to perform dangerous tasks. Expect to see a lot more of them in the future.

Medical scientists are working on **microrobots** that can be injected into patients to diagnose health issues and make repairs.

More than 10 million **robot vacuum cleaners** have been sold worldwide.

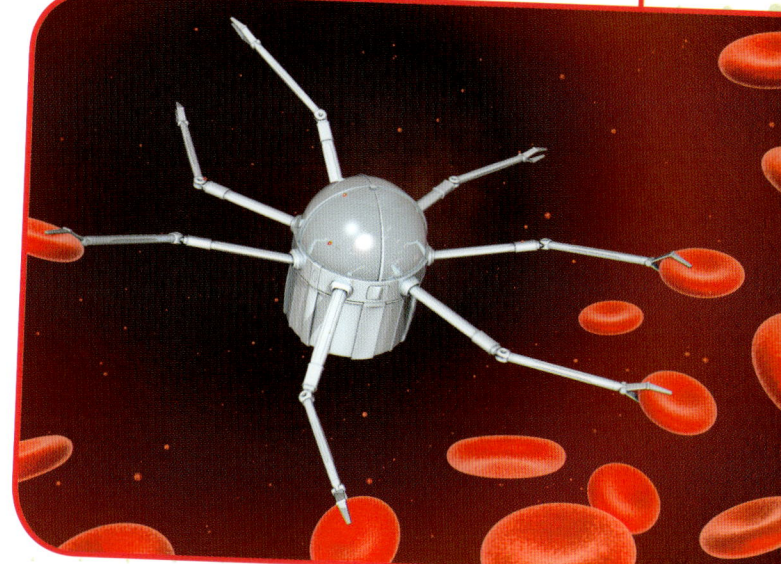

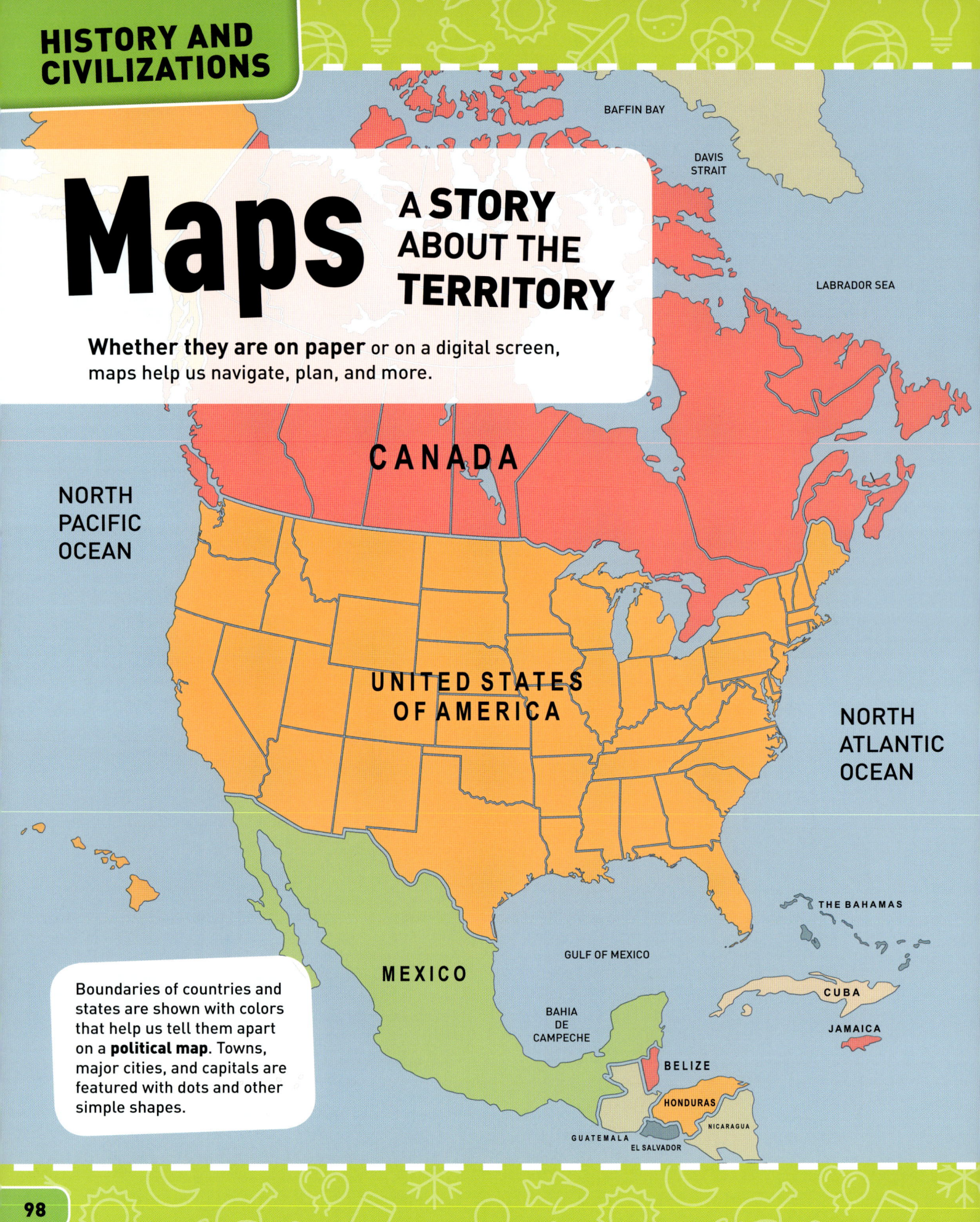

HISTORY AND CIVILIZATIONS

Maps
A STORY ABOUT THE TERRITORY

Whether they are on paper or on a digital screen, maps help us navigate, plan, and more.

Boundaries of countries and states are shown with colors that help us tell them apart on a **political map**. Towns, major cities, and capitals are featured with dots and other simple shapes.

TRAIN/SUBWAY MAP

These maps usually leave out many geographic details to present a simple outline of a transportation system. Exact paths and distances are not as important as clearly showing the train and subway routes and their relative locations.

NAVIGATIONAL CHART

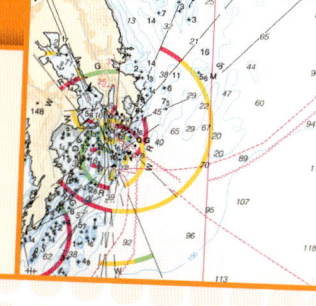

Charts present the geography of land and sea to help ships (and planes) chart a course. Obstacles, ports, and common routes are often highlighted.

THEMATIC MAP

Maps are often created to help explain a particular topic, from population growth and voting patterns to economic trends, land use, and where different languages are spoken.

STREET MAP

Detailing every street and major destination, such as parks, train stations, and other places of interest, a street map can help guide you through a city and all its neighborhoods.

ROAD MAP

Covering a wider area than a street map, a road map is all about showing streets, highways, toll roads, and their exits.

SATELLITE PHOTO

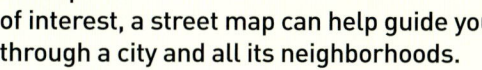

There are eyes in the sky. Today, satellites in orbit provide incredibly detailed photos that help us find our way around. They also help researchers analyze data about everything from weather to pollution.

99

HISTORY AND CIVILIZATIONS

Same World, Different Views

CHANGING OUR VIEW OF THE WORLD

The world is a sphere, of course, but most maps are flat. To present our curved planet on a rectangular surface, mapmakers must make decisions about how to fit in all the shapes and locations so that the map still resembles the actual world. So, a map can make a country seem bigger or smaller or more or less powerful than it really is.

PETERS PROJECTION

This map adjusts continents and landmasses to reflect their actual sizes relative to each other. Notice how different the continents look compared to the Mercator projection or the map in your classroom.

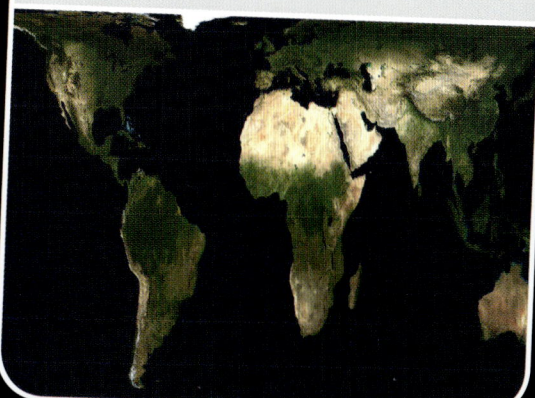

MERCATOR PROJECTION

A very popular map choice for years, this representation of the globe makes Greenland, Antarctica, and other very northern or southern land masses look much, much bigger than they actually are. It's impossible to show the north or south poles, though.

HISTORY AND CIVILIZATIONS

Waving the Flag

NATIONAL BANNERS, POWERFUL STATEMENTS

Every flag tells a story. A flag's pattern, colors, and images represent a country's history and culture. In this way, these powerful symbols bring people together. Here are some examples of how flags celebrate a sense of the past, values, and common goals.

United States
The 50 stars represent the number of states in the union. The red and white stripes represent the original 13 colonies at the time of American independence.

Ireland
The green stripe stands for the native people of Ireland, and the orange stripe represents the British who settled there. The white stripe stands for the peace between them.

Mexico
Green, white, and red represent hope, unity, and the blood of heroes. The coat of arms in the center represents Mexico's Aztec past.

Argentina
Blue is for clear skies, and white is for the snow of the Andes Mountains. The sun with a human face is the Incan sun god.

South Korea
The white background stands for peace and purity. The red and blue circle is the yin-yang symbol, representing harmony and balance. In the corners, the four trigrams (the sets of three lines) stand for heaven, earth, water, and fire.

India
The saffron stands for sacrifice, the white stands for peace, and the green stands for courage and immortality. The symbol at the center is the Ashoka Chakra. It represents righteousness, justice, and forwardness.

Australia
Britain's flag is in the top left, as Australia is part of the Commonwealth of Nations (formerly, the British Commonwealth). The points of the star below correspond to the number of original Australian states. The constellation is the Southern Cross, which is visible in the Southern Hemisphere.

Cambodia
This flag features an illustration of Angkor Wat, a Cambodian temple that is the world's largest religious monument.

Liechtenstein and Haiti
Without knowing it, Liechtenstein and Haiti designed flags that are very similar to each other. No one minded—until they competed against each other in the 1936 Olympics!

HISTORY AND CIVILIZATIONS

On the Money
CURRENCY AND COINS

Before the invention of money, people could only trade, or barter, goods and services for other goods and services. That meant you could only barter with someone if they wanted exactly what you had or could do for them. Money, or currency, allows people to buy something based on its perceived value.

Money began with shells and trinkets. Eventually, precious metals became the way to represent a measure of value.

CHINESE CURRENCY

Paper bills were first used in China around the year 900 CE. Paper currency didn't catch on in Europe until the 1600s.

GIANT COINS

Until the 1900s, enormous stone coins were used on the Pacific island of Yap. Some are as big as 12 feet (3.7 meters) across!

BIG BILL, LITTLE VALUE

In Zimbabwe in 2008, inflation (the rising cost of things) got so bad that the government had to print one hundred trillion dollar bills.

HEAVY METAL

The first known use of a precious metal as currency was about 2500 BCE in Mesopotamia (southern Iraq today). People exchanged weighted silver.

FIRST COINS

Coins were first used in what is now Turkey, around 700 BCE.

LEAF IT

British settlers used tobacco leaves as currency in North America in the 17th century because the plants grew so well in their new home and sold so well back in England.

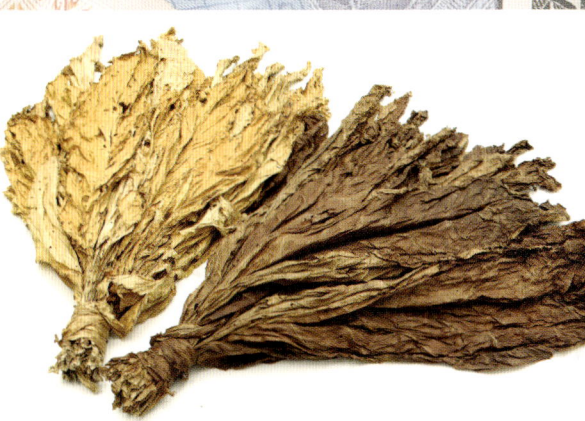

CHARGE IT!

Credit cards first came into use in the U.S. in the 1920s to purchase gas. Today, there are some businesses that only accept credit cards.

HISTORY AND CIVILIZATIONS

BORDERS AND GOVERNMENTS

Name That Country

The United States currently recognizes 195 independent world countries. The names and borders of countries often change, keeping mapmakers busy. The largest country in the world by landmass is Russia. It's pretty easy to find, but can you find the smallest country? It's Vatican City. Here's a hint: You have to look inside a larger European country to find it.

Below is a list of all the countries in the world. How many can you find?

Afghanistan
Albania
Algeria
Andorra
Angola
Antigua and Barbuda
Argentina
Armenia
Australia
Austria
Azerbaijan
Bahamas
Bahrain
Bangladesh
Barbados
Belarus
Belgium
Belize
Benin
Bhutan
Bolivia
Bosnia and Herzegovina
Botswana
Brazil
Brunei
Bulgaria
Burkina Faso
Burundi
Cabo Verde
Cambodia
Cameroon
Canada
Central African Republic (CAR)
Chad
Chile
China
Colombia
Comoros
Costa Rica
Côte d'Ivoire
Croatia
Cuba
Cyprus
Czech Republic
Democratic Republic of the Congo
Denmark
Djibouti
Dominica
Dominican Republic
Ecuador
Egypt
El Salvador
Equatorial Guinea
Eritrea
Estonia
Ethiopia
Fiji
Finland
France
Gabon
Gambia
Georgia
Germany
Ghana
Greece
Grenada
Guatemala
Guinea
Guinea-Bissau
Guyana
Haiti
Honduras
Hungary
Iceland
India
Indonesia
Iran
Iraq
Ireland
Israel
Italy
Jamaica
Japan
Jordan
Kazakhstan
Kenya
Kiribati
Kosovo
Kuwait
Kyrgyzstan
Laos
Latvia
Lebanon
Lesotho
Liberia
Libya
Liechtenstein
Lithuania
Luxembourg
Macedonia (FYROM)
Madagascar
Malawi
Malaysia
Maldives
Mali
Malta
Marshall Islands
Mauritania
Mauritius
Mexico
Micronesia
Moldova
Monaco
Mongolia
Montenegro
Morocco
Mozambique
Myanmar (Burma)
Namibia
Nauru
Nepal
Netherlands
New Zealand
Nicaragua
Niger
Nigeria
North Korea
Norway
Oman
Pakistan
Palau
Panama
Papua New Guinea
Paraguay
Peru
Philippines
Poland
Portugal
Qatar
Republic of the Congo
Romania
Russia
Rwanda
Saint Kitts and Nevis
Saint Lucia
Saint Vincent and the Grenadines
Samoa
San Marino
Sao Tome and Principe
Saudi Arabia
Senegal
Serbia
Seychelles
Sierra Leone
Singapore
Slovakia
Slovenia
Solomon Islands
Somalia
South Africa
South Korea
South Sudan
Spain
Sri Lanka
Sudan
Suriname
Swaziland
Sweden
Switzerland
Syria
Tajikistan
Tanzania
Thailand
Timor-Leste
Togo
Tonga
Trinidad and Tobago
Tunisia
Turkey
Turkmenistan
Tuvalu
Uganda
Ukraine
United Arab Emirates (UAE)
United Kingdom (UK)
United States of America (U.S.A.)
Uruguay
Uzbekistan
Vanuatu
Vatican City (Holy See)
Venezuela
Vietnam
Yemen
Zambia
Zimbabwe

HISTORY AND CIVILIZATIONS

Election Day

AWESOME AND ABSURD MOMENTS IN U.S. POLITICAL HISTORY

Democracy is part of what makes the United States of America great. And yet, there have been some pretty strange moments in American politics!

In 2016, owners of a cat named **Limberbutt McCubbins** ran their pet as a Democratic candidate for president.

During the 1872 election, **Ulysses S. Grant** ran against a dead man! His opponent, Horace Greeley, died before the election was finalized. (Grant won the election.)

Vote HAL

In 1975, students at the University of Nebraska-Lincoln ran a **computer** for student body president.

During the 1920 presidential election, a candidate, **Eugene V. Debs**, ran his campaign from prison. (He was in prison for protesting America's participation in World War I.)

In 1960 and 1972, a "UFO expert" named Gabriel Green ran for president. He claimed that his contact with **space aliens** made him qualified for the job.

DID YOU KNOW?

- American astronauts on the International Space Station can vote using a secure email connection.
- Legend says that Andrew Jackson's 1829 inauguration celebration got out of hand. Jackson was pressed against a wall by the large crowd, and the staff put tubs of drinks outside on the lawn so all the rowdy guests would leave the White House.

HISTORY AND CIVILIZATIONS

City Starters
AMAZING ANCIENT COMMUNITIES

THE CRADLE OF CIVILIZATION

The first civilizations developed between the Tigris and Euphrates rivers. This region, a part of what we now know as the Middle East, was called Mesopotamia.

The earliest ancient people were hunters and gatherers in search of food. When people found land that was good for growing crops, many of them began to farm the land, build homes, and stay in one place instead of continuing to travel. Towns sprang up and some grew into cities. The first civilizations were formed, and each had their own unique ways of building, governing, creating art, and more.

High in Peru's Andes Mountains, Machu Picchu is believed to have been a retreat for Inca rulers in the 1400s. The site was abandoned after the Incas lost power to the Spanish. It wasn't rediscovered by anyone from outside the immediate area until the late 1800s. It is sometimes called the "Lost City of the Incas."

AN ANCIENT WONDER

Ishtar Gates, Babylon

More than 3,500 years ago, Babylon was the most famous city in Mesopotamia and possibly the largest city in the world. Now, all that remains of the legendary city are ruins that lie south of Baghdad, Iraq. Spread out over nearly 4 square miles (10 square kilometers), Babylon featured a great temple and hanging gardens. The gardens were considered one of the seven wonders of the ancient world.

THE SILK ROAD

Don't let the name fool you; the Silk Road wasn't lined with silk banners. In fact, it was a group of trade routes that connected China to other places in the ancient world, including Persia and ancient Egypt. People traveled along the Silk Road to trade goods, such as gold, silver, and food for bronze, fur, and, of course, silk.

WALK LIKE AN EGYPTIAN

For more than 3,000 years, ancient Egyptian cities such as Memphis and Thebes were centers for culture and business. While pyramids are a lasting symbol of the ancient Egyptians, we have even more to thank them for. Egyptians invented the 365-days-a-year calendar, performed the world's earliest known surgeries, and even made makeup popular!

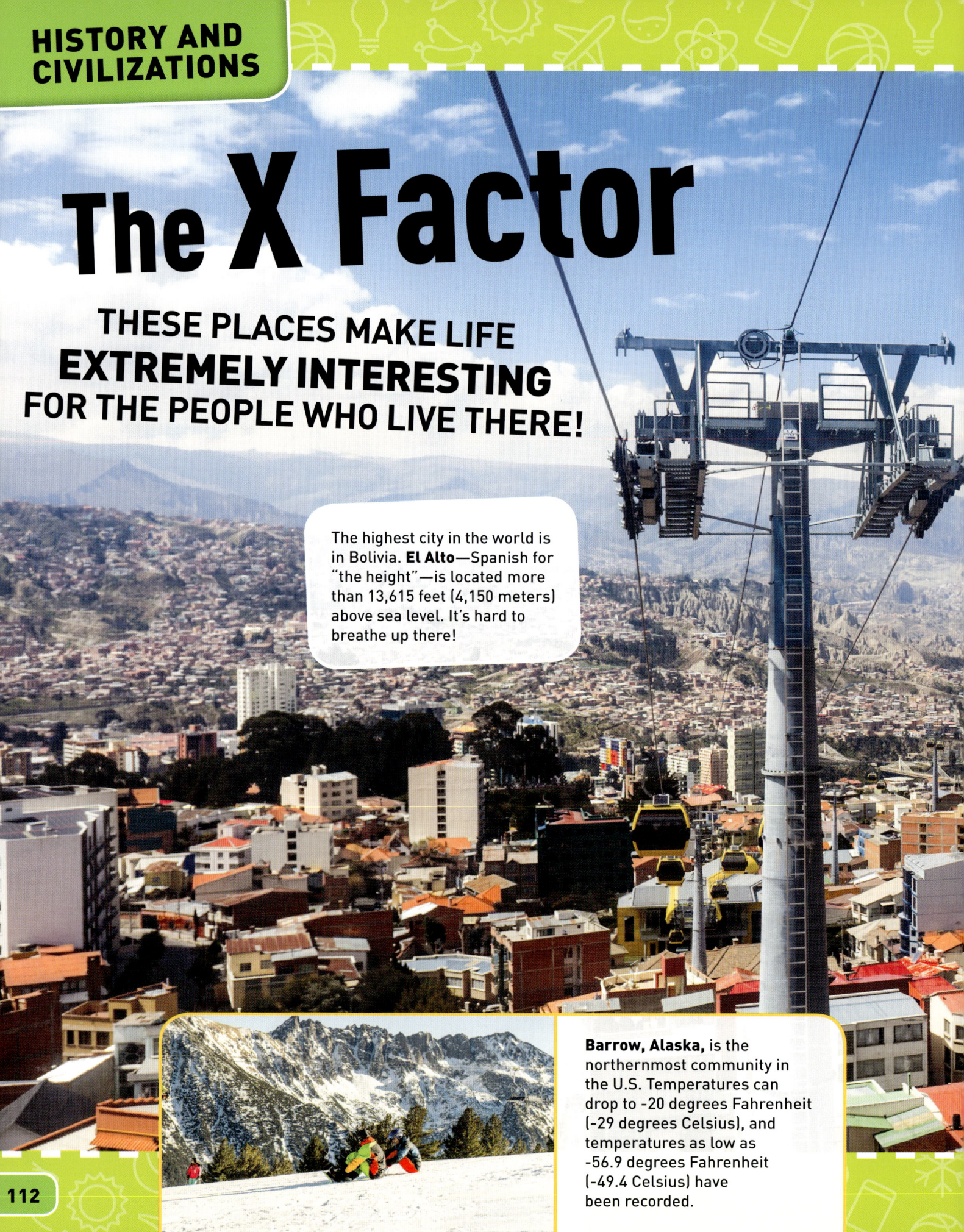

HISTORY AND CIVILIZATIONS

The X Factor

THESE PLACES MAKE LIFE EXTREMELY INTERESTING FOR THE PEOPLE WHO LIVE THERE!

The highest city in the world is in Bolivia. **El Alto**—Spanish for "the height"—is located more than 13,615 feet (4,150 meters) above sea level. It's hard to breathe up there!

Barrow, Alaska, is the northernmost community in the U.S. Temperatures can drop to -20 degrees Fahrenheit (-29 degrees Celsius), and temperatures as low as -56.9 degrees Fahrenheit (-49.4 Celsius) have been recorded.

Kuwait City, Kuwait, sets records for the world's hottest city, where temperatures have reached over 125 degrees Fahrenheit (52 degrees Celsius). In the summer, no one is allowed to work outdoors between 11:00 a.m. and 4:00 p.m.

Chicago may be known as the Windy City, but that name actually has little to do with the weather. **Wellington, New Zealand,** can steal the title. With average wind speeds of nearly 18 miles (29 kilometers) per hour, it is the windiest city in the world!

Bring your umbrella if you plan a trip to **Mawsynram, India**. This village is the world's wettest place. Every year, it can rain more than 39 feet (12 meters) there!

ARTS AND ENTERTAINMENT

An artist painted the walls of Chauvet-Pont-d'Arc Cave in France between 30,000 and 32,000 years ago. It may be the earliest example of cave art to show people or animals.

SULAWESI, INDONESIA

Scientists have recently dated images of hands and animals in a cave in south Sulawesi, Indonesia. Also in the running for the world's first pictures, they may be almost 40,000 years old.

Cave Paintings

AHEAD OF THE ART PACK

Ancient illustrations are one of the earliest signs of humanity. Painted tens of thousands of years ago, these images of people and animals have been discovered inside caves.

LASCAUX CAVE, FRANCE

More than 2,000 figures have been painted in this cave. Created about 20,000 years ago, they were the work of many artists over generations.

ALTAMIRA CAVE, SPAIN

Between 14,500 and 18,000 years ago, an artist created this charcoal drawing and color painting of local fauna.

ARTS AND ENTERTAINMENT

Vincent van Gogh
The Starry Night (1889)

Largely self-taught, Dutch painter Vincent van Gogh loved the light and colors of spring in southern France. At one point, he painted nearly one painting a day.

Georgia O'Keeffe
Jimson Weed/White Flower No. 1 (1932)

American artist Georgia O'Keeffe grew up on a farm in Wisconsin but moved to the cities of Chicago and New York to study realistic painting. She went back to nature, though, to find inspiration for her art. The painting above sold for more than $44 million in 2014, making it the world's most expensive painting by a female artist.

Michelangelo
David (circa 1501–1504)

Michelangelo Buonarroti, an Italian painter, architect, sculptor, and poet, started his career at age 13, working as an apprentice to a famous painter. While Michelangelo is probably best known for his painting on the ceiling of the Sistine Chapel, he considered sculpting marble his life's main work.

DID YOU KNOW?

- Michelangelo complained to a friend about the physical pain of working on the Sistine Chapel, calling it torture. He wrote, "I am not in the right place—I am not a painter."
- Leonardo da Vinci was known for being an extremely slow painter, and many of his paintings were never finished.
- Hokusai's *The Great Wave* was the inspiration for a famous musical masterpiece—Claude Debussy's *La Mer* (The Sea).

The Masterpiece
EXPRESSING THOUGHTS, FEELINGS, AND DESIRES THROUGH ART

Since the first cave painters, artists have found ways to communicate with others and share the ways they experience the world by drawing, painting, sculpting, and creating works of art. Some artists create masterpieces that people enjoy and study for centuries.

Katsushika Hokusai
The Great Wave off Kanagawa (circa 1826–1833)

Leonardo da Vinci
Mona Lisa (circa 1503–1519)

As a young man, Japanese artist Katsushika Hokusai learned to carve art into wood blocks, which were then coated with ink to make prints. He is famous for his work in this style, but he also created huge public paintings that measured up to 600 feet (180 meters) long.

Known for his passion and genius in the worlds of both art and science, Da Vinci spent his life observing, inventing, and creating art. He filled notebook pages with thousands of sketches as he studied subjects such as the human body, the motion of water, and flight.

ARTS AND ENTERTAINMENT

Celebrated Styles

FAMOUS STYLES OF MODERN ART

The term "modern art" generally refers to works created from the 1860s through the 1970s. During that time, traditions of the past were left behind and experimentation ruled the day.

IMPRESSIONISM

The broad brushstrokes capture a feeling of the moment rather than precise details.

Claude Monet
Water Lilies
(1916)

SURREALISM

Fantastic images are used to create art that seems like it came from a dream.

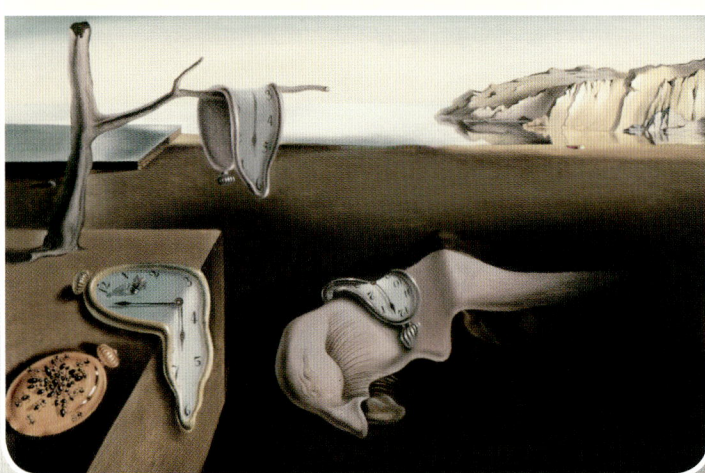

Salvador Dalí
The Persistence of Memory
(1931)

ABSTRACT ART

Abstract artists paint shapes and colors that don't have to be recognizable things.

Wassily Kandinsky
Composition 8
(1923)

POINTILLISM

Artists combine tiny dots to create new colors and shapes that reveal themselves from a distance.

Georges-Pierre Seurat
A Sunday Afternoon on the Island of La Grande Jatte
(1884–1886)

DADA

Everyday objects are used to present art in new and unusual ways.

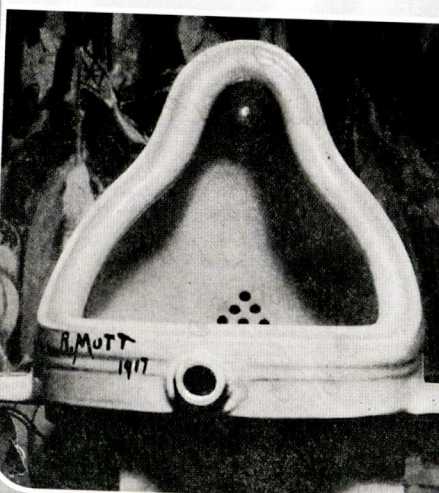

Marcel Duchamp
Fountain
(1917, replica 1964)

ABSTRACT EXPRESSIONISM

Abstract expressionists don't try to paint what they see in the real world. They focus on the physical qualities of paint and freely use a wide range of techniques to express a strong sense of emotion.

Jackson Pollock
Reflection of the Big Dipper
(1947)

CUBISM

Many different points of view are combined in a single image.

Pablo Picasso
Harlequin Musician
(1924)

119

ARTS AND ENTERTAINMENT

The Romani people migrated to the Andalusian region of Spain in the 1400s. They brought their instruments—tambourines, bells, and wooden castanets. They also brought their own styles of music and dance. Over time, those styles began to blend with the folk music traditions of the Andalusian Jews, Muslims, and Christians. By the 1700s, this musical mixing had created the style of music and dance called **flamenco**.

The Music Makers

COMMUNICATE WITH MUSIC!

THE PAST MEETS THE PRESENT

In the African country of Senegal, musicians took the traditional storytelling songs of the Wolof people and mixed them with modern styles of jazz, funk, pop, and Latin music to create a new style of music called mbalax. The artist Youssou N'Dour took his upbeat, danceable mbalax tunes and shared them with the world.

DID YOU KNOW?

- Do you feel like your heartbeat changes when you listen to a song? That's because it does— it mimics the tempo, or speed, of the music!
- Some scientific studies have found that classical music helps plants grow. Others have found that listening to symphonies helps your brain focus.
- The composer Mozart had perfect pitch, or the ability to recognize or repeat a musical note without a reference. The jazz singer Ella Fitzgerald did, too. Perfect pitch is rare, though. Studies say only 1 in 10,000 people have it. Do you?

A folk instrument, **bagpipes** have been played for thousands of years but are most associated with Scottish history. Scotland's national instrument, bagpipes were traditionally used by the Scots to inspire soldiers and scare off enemies on the battlefield.

ARTS AND ENTERTAINMENT

WEIRD AND WACKY WAYS TO MAKE MUSIC

Extraordinary Notes

PUMP UP THE VOLUME

R.E. Bates thought the acoustic guitar sounded sweet but lacked power. That's why he invented the harpitar. To make it, he took the body of a harp and strung six strings across its center, as if it were a guitar.

MUSIC GOOD ENOUGH TO EAT

People have turned fruits and vegetables into musical instruments: gourd maracas, sweet-potato whistles, coconut thumb pianos, and carrot clarinets! There's even a whole orchestra that makes music with food—the Vienna Vegetable Orchestra!

TAP, TAP

Alexander Rose wrote a song that is played by typing words on a musical typewriter. In 1938, he invented the Typatune, which has a typewriter-style keyboard. When you tap a key, it hits a string inside the instrument, just like a piano!

KEY OF SEA

You probably know wind instruments like the tuba and trombone, but have you ever tried playing a mollusk shell? You can even listen to a musician play lead conch in a shell choir!

123

ARTS AND ENTERTAINMENT

1800
Loose, free-flowing dresses mimicked the clothing styles of ancient Greece.

1837
In the early Victorian era, corsets were wound so tightly around women's waists that they could hardly breathe. Giant hoop skirts were also popular.

1810 1820 1830 1840 1850 1860 1870

1920
The end of World War I and the signing of the 19th Amendment of the U.S. Constitution, which gave women the right to vote, launched some dramatic fashion changes. Flappers cut their hair short and wore shorter dresses.

1950
Teen fashion trends started when movie stars like James Dean and rock stars like Elvis Presley rose in popularity.

1880 1890 1900 1910 1920 1930 1940

Fashion Forward

TRENDS IN CLOTHING

1984
Colorful clothes, dangly jewelry, and big hair were fashion trends.

1990
Flannel shirts, ripped jeans, and Doc Martens® became the uniform of the grunge music movement.

1967
The Summer of Love launched a social movement as well as a fashion trend. Hippies let their free-spirited selves show in their clothing choices.

2000
As people wanted to be more comfortable at play and at work, performance fabrics became popular.

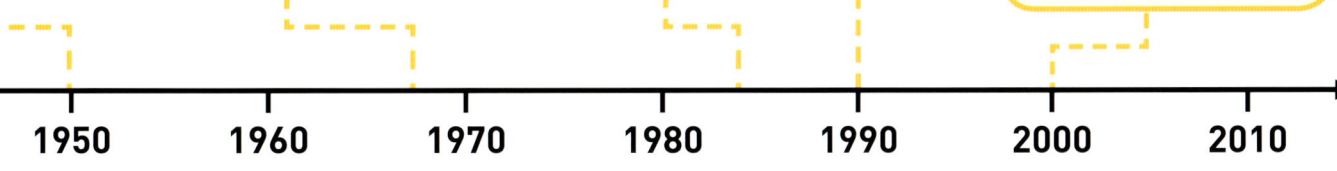

1950   1960   1970   1980   1990   2000   2010

ARTS AND ENTERTAINMENT

These Shoes Are Made for Walking

WHY SHOES WERE INVENTED

For thousands of years, people have been covering their feet to protect them. Along the way, shoemakers started getting fashionable, making shoes with all kinds of materials and in all kinds of styles. Here are some interesting shoe fashions.

FUN FACTS!

- What's in a shoe size? Each size is equal to the diameter of 1 barleycorn, or 0.3 inches (0.8 centimeters). King Edward II of England established that measurement.
- Sneakers got their name because their rubber soles make them quiet.
- High-heeled shoes were originally designed for short men.

126

Hundreds of years ago in the Ottoman Empire, wealthy women wore stilt-like shoes, called **qabaqib**, to protect their feet from the hot, wet floors of public baths. The wooden shoes were bridge-shaped and decorated with mother-of-pearl or silver.

This boot print was made by Neil Armstrong, the first person to walk on the Moon. Today, an MIT student is designing **space boots** for the first people to walk on Mars!

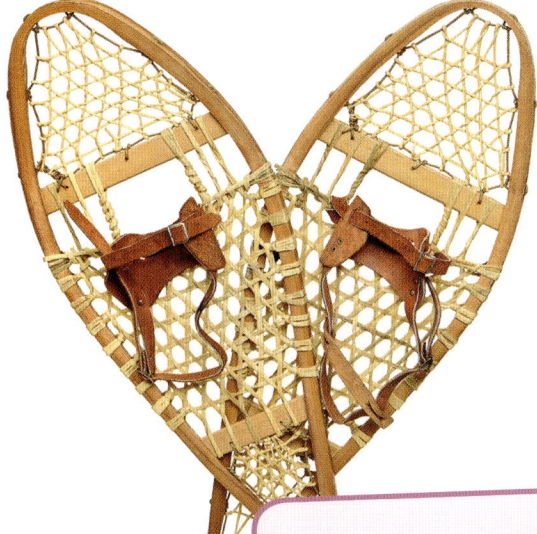

The earliest **snowshoes** were slabs of wood tied to the bottom of the wearer's feet. When the frames were built of flexible wood and laces were added, it became even easier to move along the top of snow.

Covered with red sequins, these shoes have danced down the Yellow Brick Road and can now be found in Smithsonian's National Museum of American History. In L. Frank Baum's book *The Wonderful Wizard of Oz* and in the film's original script, Dorothy Gale's **ruby-red slippers** were silver. Several pairs of the famous shoes were made for the movie.

ARTS AND ENTERTAINMENT

A **fascinator hat** is small and fancy. It is usually held in place by a headband or comb and can be decorated with feathers, beads, or flowers. The term was first used in the U.S. in the 1860s; in the early 1900s, fascinator wearers started sporting some really wild hat designs. Some fascinators even had whole stuffed birds on them!

The **New York Easter Parade** started in the late 1800s. Today, many people come out just for the fashion, especially the hats!

Cowboy hats may seem as American as baseball, but they were first worn by horsemen in Mongolia in the 13th century. The wide-brim hats help to keep the sun's glare out of a cowboy's eyes. In winter, the tall crown of the hat keeps a cowboy's head warm. A cowboy can even fill up his hat with water to give his horse a drink!

Baseball caps are worn by a lot of people who never play the game. The first baseball team, the Knickerbockers, wore straw hats! It was only in the 1860s when caps showed up with round tops and big visors. They were worn by a team named the Brooklyn Excelsiors. The Brooklyn-style caps soon caught on throughout the major leagues—and everywhere else!

A chef's hat, called a **toque**, traditionally has 100 folds. Each fold represents one way to cook an egg.

President Abraham Lincoln's **stovepipe hat** made him stand out from the crowd. Besides wearing it on his head, he also used it to store notes and important papers!

Hats Off to... HATS!

ONE FOR EVERY HEAD!

From the Cat in the Hat's red-and-white-striped stovepipe to the Mad Hatter's green top hat, hats can be as colorful as the characters who wear them.

DID YOU KNOW?

A cave in western France contains ancient drawings of humans—and some of them are wearing hats. The carvings on the floor of **La Marche cave** could be 15,000 years old!

ARTS AND ENTERTAINMENT

3000 BCE

Checkers and chess have been around for a long time, but the oldest known board game comes from ancient Egypt around 5,000 years ago. Two people play the game of senet, which means "passing," by throwing four two-sided sticks in order to take a turn. The game board has 30 squares, some with symbols on them. The symbols tell whether the player has good or bad luck.

2100 BCE

1905

Does a story that involves revenge, betrayal, a long journey, a power-hungry king, and a battle against a terrifying monster sound familiar? Before the days of superhero movies and fantasy television shows, epic stories were told out loud and passed down from generation to generation. Dated from around 2100 BCE, *The Epic of Gilgamesh*, a long poem from ancient Mesopotamia, is one of the oldest survivors of this storytelling tradition. It tells about the adventures of Gilgamesh, a Sumerian king.

In 1905, the nickelodeon opened its doors to the people of Pittsburgh, Pennsylvania. For a nickel, they could visit one of the first theaters dedicated to moving-picture shows and watch a 12-minute movie called *The Great Train Robbery*. It was projected by a cinematograph, a machine invented by two French brothers, Auguste and Louis Lumière.

According to one recent survey, more than 118 million U.S. homes have televisions. It's hard to even imagine a time when home televisions weren't popular, but there are plenty of people around today who remember that time. In the 1940s and 1950s, many of the first TV shows, such as *The Lone Ranger* and *Adventures of Superman*, began as popular radio shows.

1949

That's Entertainment!

FILL YOUR FREE TIME WITH FUN!

What did ancient people do when they weren't busy hunting and gathering? They told stories, played board games, and invented some of the sports we play today.

1935

Virtual reality may seem like a new form of entertainment, but it actually has a long history. In his 1935 story "Pygmalion's Spectacles," writer Stanley G. Weinbaum imagined a pair of goggles that would let the wearer see, hear, smell, taste, and touch a fictional world. Imagine if he could put on a pair of today's VR goggles!

ARTS AND ENTERTAINMENT

A Round of Applause

ARE YOU NOT **ENTERTAINED**?

Performers display their wide range of talents to put on a thrilling show.

Harry Houdini, world-famous magician and escape artist, reached the height of his career by hanging upside down. In his Chinese Water Torture Cell act, Houdini was lowered by his feet into a water-filled cabinet. Hidden from the audience and claiming to be underwater, he would take three minutes to escape, holding his breath the entire time.

Cirque du Soleil started as a band of roaming performers in a small village in Quebec, Canada. Today, the company puts on 22 spectacular shows all over the world.

Known almost as well for his spectacular crashes as for his death-defying stunts, **Evel Knievel** holds the record for the most broken bones in a lifetime—433 in total!

Circus contortionists twist their limbs in ways most people find unimaginable. As a member of a legendary English circus family, Rose Julian started performing with the Julian Acrobats in the 1870s, when she was only eight years old. She was known as the greatest contortionist of the time.

ARTS AND ENTERTAINMENT

It's Crowded in Here

THE POWER OF THE PEOPLE

Amazing things happen when groups of people gather!

Pink Running Day is a ladies-only event held in Rotterdam, Netherlands. The runners race different distances to raise money for the Pink Ribbon Foundation, which helps support women who have been affected by breast cancer. Each year, there are pink runs and walks all over the world to fight breast cancer.

Flash mob celebrating Russia Day in Volgograd, Russia

Originally intended as a kind of performance art, a **flash mob** is a large, sudden gathering of people who perform an unusual act and then quickly scatter. Bill Wasik, a magazine editor, organized the first successful flash mob at a Macy's department store in New York City in 2003. They are often organized on social media and kept a secret. Some flash mobs dance, some sing, and some throw colors into the air!

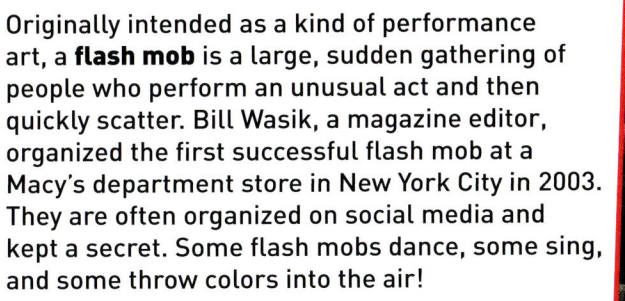

The **ALS Ice Bucket Challenge** was a charitable social-media campaign that went viral in the summer of 2014. More than 17 million people posted videos of themselves getting dunked with ice water. The videos raised money for the ALS Association, which raises money to help people living with the disease amyotrophic lateral sclerosis (ALS). The campaign worked! More than $100 million was raised in a month. Some of that money helped fund the researchers who identified a new gene associated with the disease. This discovery could lead to new forms of treatment!

ARTS AND ENTERTAINMENT

Dance With Me

LET YOUR BODY MOVE TO THE MUSIC!

From tap to tango, people use dance to express themselves creatively.

Break-dancing was invented in the 1970s in the Bronx, a borough of New York City. The hip-hop dance style features four basic dance elements. "Toprock" is done from a standing position and includes shuffles and foot moves. "Downrock" is performed with the hands and feet on the ground. "Freezes" are, well, just what they sound like: frozen body positions. Finally, "power moves" are acrobatic spins on the floor and in the air.

DID YOU KNOW?

- Research has shown that dancing is good for your physical and mental health! It lowers your risk of dying from heart disease and improves your brain function.
- Found at two 9,000-year-old sites in Turkey and Jordan, engraved stone and rock carvings depict what look like dancing figures. They are thought to be the oldest evidence of dancing.
- The longest dance marathon for a single person lasted more than five days!
- In 1988, nearly 120,000 people in Miami set the world record for the longest conga line.

Bollywood—a term that combines "Bombay" (the city now known as Mumbai) and "Hollywood"—refers to India's Hindi-language film industry. Bollywood films are known for their popular dance scenes, which often mix Western styles with traditional forms of Indian dance and music.

Ballroom dancing has become a serious competitive sport, with dancers from roughly 30 countries competing in international competitions every year. It's even recognized by the International Olympic Committee!

A truly American art form, **tap dancing** was created from a combination of Scottish, English, and Irish clog dances and African tribal dances.

It is believed that, in 1832, Marie Taglioni became the first **ballet dancer** to use pointe shoes. These leather-soled satin slippers weren't as strong as modern pointe shoes, but they were reinforced on the tips and sides.

ARTS AND ENTERTAINMENT

A Walk in the Park

THAT'S WHERE THE FUN IS!

For centuries, carnivals and traveling fairs have rolled into town and brought fun to crowds of all ages. Theme parks and amusement parks turned that idea around: They let people roll to the fun any time they want!

Roller coasters are thrilling—and the perfect place to see the laws of physics at work! Most roller coasters use only one motor to pull the cars up to the top of the first hill. The rest of the ride is powered by gravity.

During the golden age of carousels, from 1870 to 1930, nearly 4,000 **merry-go-rounds** were built with wooden animals carved and painted by artists. Today, the horses and other animals that ride around and around are mostly made from aluminum and fiberglass.

The **carousel** is one of the oldest amusement park rides, dating back to around 500 CE. Drawings show riders of the first carousels circling around a post in baskets—like the carousel swing pictured, just a lot closer to the ground.

Ferris wheels are named for their inventor, bridge builder and engineer George Washington Ferris Jr. For the 1893 Chicago World's Fair, he designed a 264-foot (80-meter) wheel that could carry up to 2,160 riders at a time.

DID YOU KNOW?

The best way to battle motion sickness is to ride on a lot of fast-spinning rides. Eventually, the system in your body that controls balance will become desensitized.

ARTS AND ENTERTAINMENT

Mark That Date!

THERE ARE PLENTY OF REASONS TO CELEBRATE ALL YEAR LONG!

Be sure to mark your favorite days on your own calendar.

December 4
National Sock Day

January
- 1 Global Family Day
- 4 World Braille Day
- 11 International Thank-You Day
- **14 National Dress Up Your Pet Day**
- 19 National Popcorn Day

February
- 8 National Kite-Flying Day
- 17 National Random Acts of Kindness Day
- 22 World Thinking Day
- 24 National Tortilla Chip Day
- **27 National Polar Bear Day**

March
- 3 National Anthem Day
- **7 National Cereal Day**
- 13 National Earmuff Day
- 19 National Let's Laugh Day
- 20 World Frog Day
- 22 World Water Day

April
- **4 National School Librarian Day**
- 11 National Pet Day
- 21 International Creativity and Innovation Day
- 22 Earth Day
- 25 World Penguin Day

May
- 1 National Mother Goose Day
- 5 National Astronaut Day
- 10 National Clean Up Your Room Day
- 25 World Turtle Day
- **28 National Hamburger Day**

June
- 1 National Say Something Nice Day
- **8 National Best Friends Day**
- 14 National Strawberry Shortcake Day
- 30 National Meteor Watch Day

March 13 National Earmuff Day

July
- **6 National Fried Chicken Day**
- 8 World Ocean Day
- 11 World Population Day
- 13 National French Fry Day
- 16 World Snake Day
- 24 National Cousins Day

August
- 6 National Wiggle Your Toes Day
- 10 National Lazy Day
- 13 International Lefthanders Day
- 14 World Lizard Day
- **26 National Cherry Popsicle Day**

September
- 6 National Read a Book Day
- 8 International Literacy Day
- 13 International Chocolate Day
- 18 National Cheeseburger Day
- 19 Talk Like a Pirate Day
- **25 National Comic Book Day**

October
- 4 World Animal Day
- 16 National Dictionary Day
- **21 National Reptile Awareness Day**
- 31 National Knock-Knock Jokes Day

November
- 6 National Saxophone Day
- **10 National Vanilla Cupcake Day**
- 17 National Take a Hike Day
- 19 National Play Monopoly Day
- 21 World Television Day
- 28 National French Toast Day

December
- 4 National Sock Day
- 5 International Volunteers Day
- **13 National Violin Day**
- 21 National Crossword Puzzle Day
- 30 National Bacon Day

ARTS AND ENTERTAINMENT

Funfest
CELEBRATE THE WEIRD AND WACKY

There's a festival for anything you can imagine—you just have to know where to find it.

Thousands of lanterns light the night at the **Yi Peng Lantern Festival**, in Chiang Mai, Thailand. The floating lanterns are released into the sky, a symbol of letting go of all the year's bad luck.

When most people hear buzzing mosquitoes, they want to swat them away, not celebrate them. At the **Great Texas Mosquito Festival**, you can join a mosquito-calling contest and meet Willie Man-Chew, the mosquito mascot!

If you have a fear of heights, stay away from the **Highline Meeting**, near Misurina, Italy. Highlining is an extreme form of "slacklining," where people walk along a length of thin, flat material suspended between two elevated points, high above the ground or water.

People use duct tape to make wallets, wrap presents, and even build boats. The **Avon Heritage Duck Tape Festival**—named because some folks mistakenly refer to duct tape as "duck" tape— celebrates this sticky substance in Avon, Ohio.

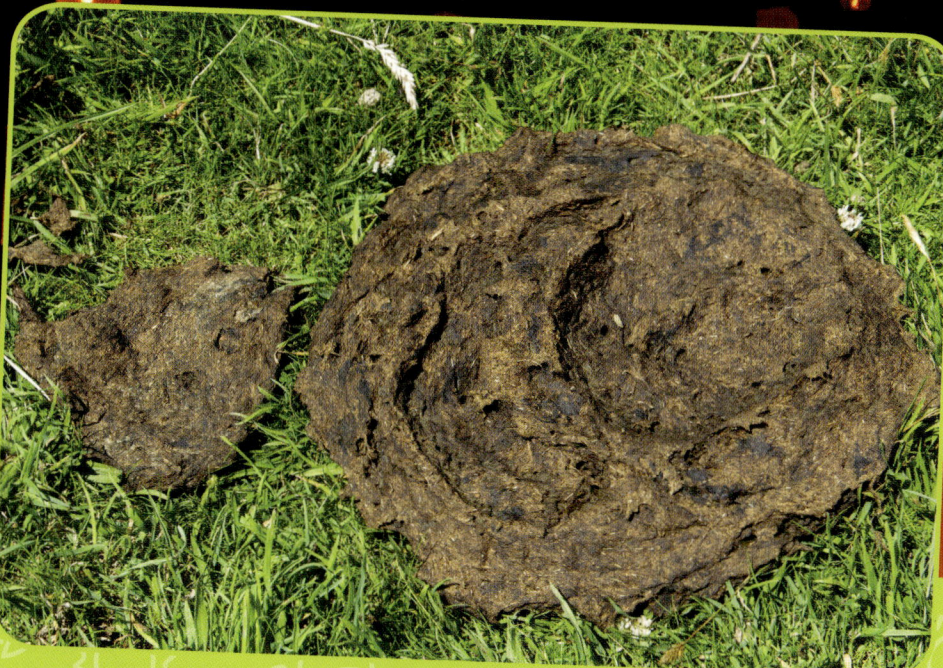

Cow chips aren't a tasty beef snack; they're actually big, dried pieces of cow poop. Every Labor Day weekend, people head to the **Wisconsin State Cow-Chip Throw and Festival**. The record for tossing a cow chip is 248 feet (76 meters)!

ARTS AND ENTERTAINMENT

There's a Museum for That?

AWESOME AND **UNUSUAL** EXHIBITIONS

Around the world, historians, collectors, and, yes, some oddballs have assembled some incredible collections. Here are a few of the world's weirdest museums.

It's hard to believe that a museum dedicated to toilets and sanitation would make the pages of a news publication. But in 2014, *Time* magazine named the Sulabh International Museum of Toilets, in New Delhi, India, as one of the weirdest in the world. Once there, you can see a toilet that is disguised as a bookcase and a replica of the throne-like chamber pot used by King Louis XIV of France.

People visit museums to see great masterpieces and giant dinosaur fossils. However, if you don't visit La Crosse to see the **Kansas Barbed Wire Museum**, you might never know how interesting barbed wire really is. For example, barbed wire fencing helped tame the Wild West by making it possible for ranchers to cheaply fence in their cattle, putting an end to the days when cowboys watched herds roam on the open range.

Allen Woodall loved metal lunch boxes so much, he turned his collection into a museum. At his Columbus, Georgia, **Lunch Box Museum**, you can see more than 1,000 lunch boxes with pop-culture icons such as King Kong, Mary Poppins, and Luke Skywalker.

The city of Ikeda, Japan, is the birthplace of instant noodles and the home of the **Momofuku Ando Instant Ramen Museum**. There, you'll learn about the origin of ramen, see actual vacuum-packed ramen made for an astronaut, and test your knowledge of instant noodles.

The **Mummy Museum** of Guanajuato, Mexico, might seem a little ghoulish. It's filled with history—and dead bodies. Unlike most ancient Egyptian mummies, these bodies were mummified through a natural process, most likely because of the area's special climate.

WORDS AND LANGUAGE

Hello | Hola | Bonjour | こんにちは

Everybody's Talking

AWESOME LANGUAGES

Written, spoken, or texted—language is one of the abilities that make humans unique in the world.

Some scientists estimate that language began around 100,000 years ago, about the time that humans developed the vocal chords we still use.

Today, about 7,000 languages are spoken around the world. This number keeps changing as we identify new languages. At the same time, many languages are falling out of use and vanishing forever as people stop using them. In fact, every couple of weeks, another language vanishes.

THE UNITED LANGUAGES OF AMERICA

More than 300 different languages are spoken in the United States. About one-fifth of U.S. residents speak a language other than English at home.

LANGUAGES AROUND THE WORLD

- **Chinese:** There isn't one single spoken Chinese language. Mandarin, one of about 10 major varieties of Chinese, is the official national language of China. With more than a billion native speakers, Chinese is the most widely spoken language on the planet.
- **Spanish:** Spanish has around 400 million native speakers. It is the main language in 21 countries, from Ecuador to Equatorial Guinea.
- **English:** There are about 375 million native English speakers around the world, but over a billion people speak the language worldwide. It is also the most used language on the Internet.
- **Hindi and Bengali:** With as many as 400 million Hindi speakers and 200 million Bengali speakers, Hindi and Bengali are the two most spoken languages in India.
- **Portuguese:** More than 200 million people speak Portuguese as their native language. While Portugal is a small country today, its language was spread far and wide during past ages of exploration and colonization.
- **French:** More than 77 million people speak French as their native language. In the past, French was considered the language of diplomacy because so many different people could use it to communicate.

DID YOU KNOW?

More than 800 different languages are spoken among Papua New Guinea's regions and their communities.

WORDS AND LANGUAGE

Phloem Bundles
Strands of plant matter left over from peeling a banana

You Don't Say!

UNCOMMON WORDS FOR EVERYDAY THINGS

"Check your aglets."
"Don't forget your tittles!"

Our world is full of things that have their own special names—ones that you probably didn't know existed at all!

Ferrule
The metal ring at the end of a pencil that holds the eraser

Lemniscate
The infinity symbol

Aglets
The plastic tips on the ends of shoelaces

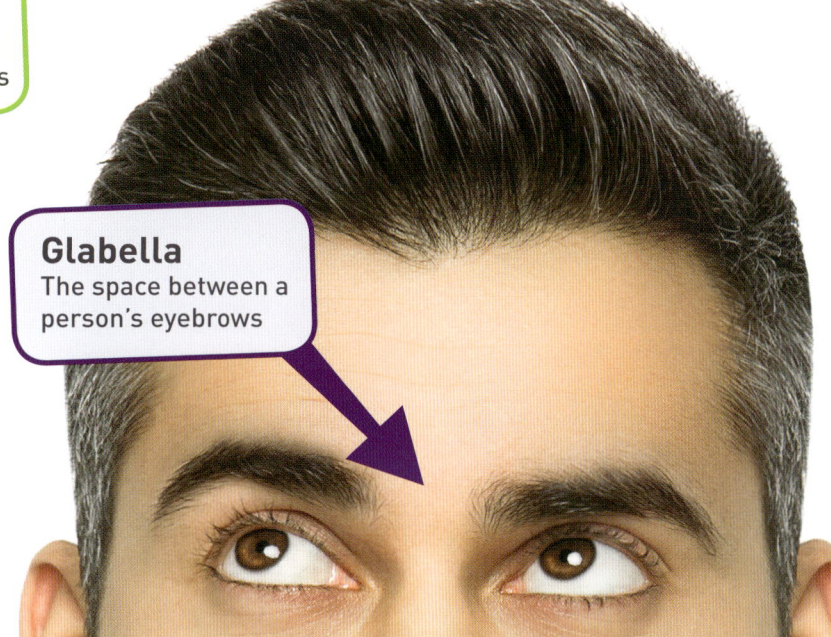

Griffonage
Sloppy, hard-to-read handwriting

Tittle
The dot over the letters *i* or *j*

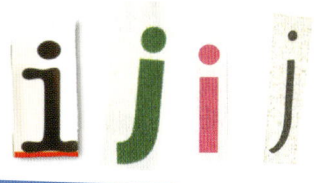

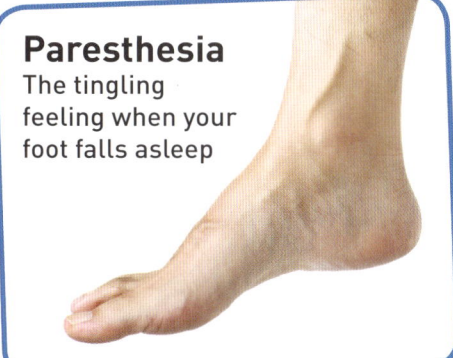

Paresthesia
The tingling feeling when your foot falls asleep

Glabella
The space between a person's eyebrows

WORDS AND LANGUAGE

Top Secret!

THE WORLD OF CODES AND CIPHERS

As long as people have been communicating, they've had a need to keep their conversations secret. From the simple switching of symbols to sophisticated digital cryptography, people have used codes and ciphers to send and disguise information.

THE PIGPEN CIPHER

Also known as the Masonic cipher or tic-tac-toe cipher, letters are represented by pieces of a grid.

CODE OR CIPHER?

A code is a method of disguising or shortening a message by substituting a word or phrase for a different word or phrase. A cipher is a method of substituting or scrambling the individual characters, letters, or groups of letters in a message. To understand a code, you usually need a codebook with a list of substitutions. Ciphers, on the other hand, usually use mathematical formulas. Most of the time, when people say "code," they mean "cipher."

THE CAESAR CIPHER

Also known as the shift cipher, this method of concealing information dates back to at least the time of Julius Caesar (around 50 BCE). Using a wheel or other device, letters of the alphabet are shifted to represent other letters.

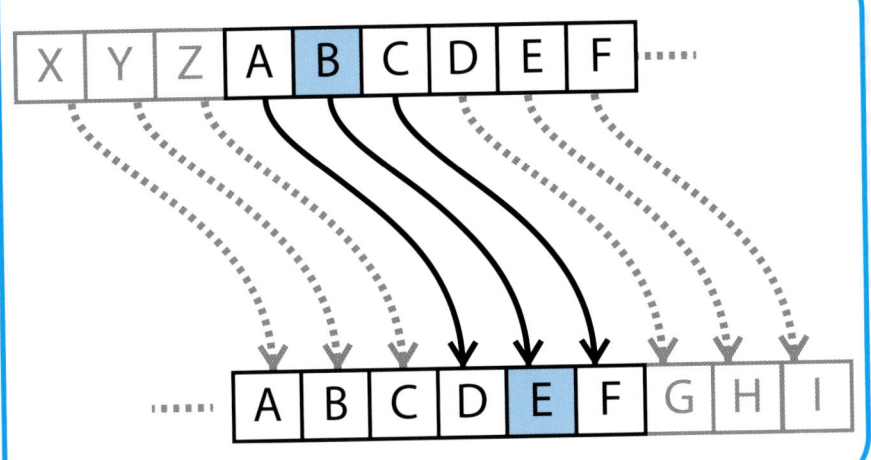

THE ENIGMA MACHINE

During World War II, the German army used the Enigma cipher to transmit their military plans to one another. Polish and British scientists created new ways of breaking the cipher—and this led to the invention of the computer!

MORSE CODE

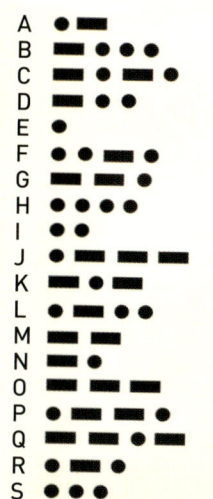
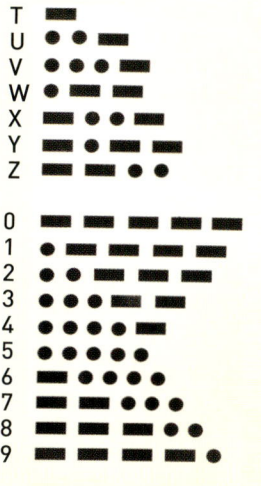

In this way of transmitting text, letters are substituted by sequences of short dots or long dashes. This actually wasn't intended to hide secrets; it was used to send messages by telegraph, the first system of electrical communication.

WORDS AND LANGUAGE

Hieroglyphs
THE **WRITING** ON THE WALL

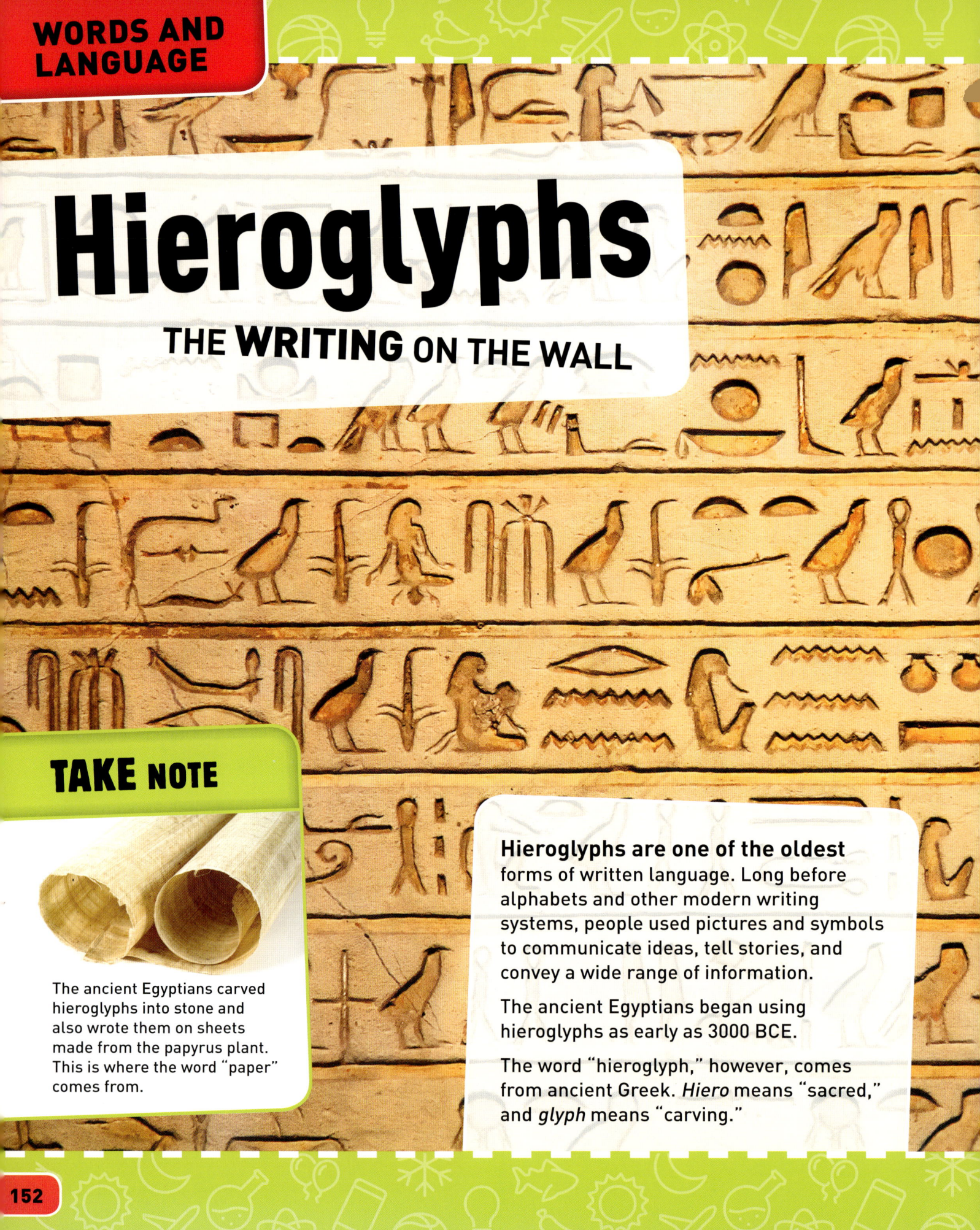

TAKE NOTE

The ancient Egyptians carved hieroglyphs into stone and also wrote them on sheets made from the papyrus plant. This is where the word "paper" comes from.

Hieroglyphs are one of the oldest forms of written language. Long before alphabets and other modern writing systems, people used pictures and symbols to communicate ideas, tell stories, and convey a wide range of information.

The ancient Egyptians began using hieroglyphs as early as 3000 BCE.

The word "hieroglyph," however, comes from ancient Greek. *Hiero* means "sacred," and *glyph* means "carving."

THE ROSETTA STONE

In 1799, French soldiers found a stone in the city of Rosetta (Rashid), Egypt. This stone had the same message written in both hieroglyphs and Greek. It was an incredible translation tool that helped archaeologists unlock the meaning of ancient Egyptian writing.

WHAT DO THE PICTURES MEAN?

Each single image could stand for a word, called a logogram, or a sound, called a phonogram. For example, we might understand that a picture of an eye could mean the word "eye" or the sound of the letter "i."

BACK TO THE BEGINNING?

Today, people use emojis to communicate on their mobile devices. Once again, simple pictures convey a wide range of ideas. Has human written communication come full circle?

WORDS AND LANGUAGE

My Word!

AWESOME TRICKS AND FUN WITH WORDS AND LANGUAGE

The English language (and all other languages, for that matter) is like a set of playing pieces you can use to create all kinds of puzzles, games, and clever tricks with words.

Enjoy these examples, then make your own!

SPOONERISM

A spoonerism is a funny way to mix up language—you switch the initial sounds of two words.

Pickled tink

Go shake a tower

Don't sweat the petty things, and don't pet the sweaty things!

May I take your coat?

May I tote your cake?

REBUS

A rebus is when you create words or phrases using pictures and symbols.

Top: I ate fish.

Bottom: Can you see?

PALINDROME

Palindromes are words or sentences that are exactly the same forward and backward. The word kayak is a palindrome. Here are some more.

Madam, I'm Adam.

Was it a rat I saw?

Mr. Owl ate my metal worm.

A man, a plan, a canal—Panama!

OXYMORON

Oxymorons are words or phrases that contradict each other. How many of these have you used?

Jumbo shrimp	**Even odds**
Pretty ugly	**Civil war**
Crash landing	**Ill health**
Freezer burn	**Old news**
Student teacher	**Terribly good**

TOM SWIFTY

A Tom Swifty is a pun that's made by taking a quoted sentence and adding an adverb, a word that modifies a verb or another adverb, to describe the way it was said by the speaker. The adverb needs to match the sentence in clever ways.

"I'm so thirsty," he said dryly.

"It's freezing in here," she said coldly.

"I don't know which groceries to buy," she said listlessly.

WORDS AND LANGUAGE

What's in a Name?

HELLO my name is

ORIGINAL MEANINGS OF POPULAR AMERICAN LAST NAMES

Last names, or surnames, became common in English around 1400 CE. Many of them have their origins in occupations and locations. If your last name is Taylor, chances are that someone in your family history was a maker of clothes. Here are some common names and where they may have started.

Wang
This popular Chinese name means "king."

Baker
You got it—someone who bakes

Sawyer
A lumber worker, or a "sawyer" of wood

Mendoza
This name evolved from the words "cold mountain" in the Basque language.

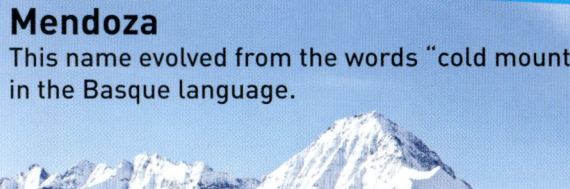

Fletcher
Someone who makes or sells arrows

Rossi
Rossi comes from the Italian word for red.

Bailey
A porter, or someone who carries things

Novak
The most popular last name from Slavic countries, including Poland and Romania, means "newcomer" or "stranger."

Smith
A blacksmith, or someone who works with metal

WORDS AND LANGUAGE

Quite a Mouthful!

SOME REALLY, REALLY LONG WORDS TO TWIST YOUR TONGUE

CAN I JUST CALL YOU ADOLPH?

A German-American man, born in 1914, had the name Adolph Blaine Charles David Earl Frederick Gerald Hubert Irvin John Kenneth Lloyd Martin Nero Oliver Paul Quincy Randolph Sherman Thomas Uncas Victor William Xerxes Yancy Wolfeschlegelsteinhausenbergerdorff Sr.!

Here are some words that you might not want to use if you're in a hurry!

Pneumonoultramicroscopicsilicovolcanoconiosis
Meaning: an alternate name for silicosis, a lung disease
It is the longest word in the English language to be published in major dictionaries. It was invented by the National Puzzlers' League in 1935 for the purpose of creating a long word.

Honorificabilitudinitatibus
Meaning: able to achieve honors
It is the longest word used by William Shakespeare, from his play *Love's Labour's Lost*.

Antidisestablishmentarianism
Meaning: being against taking away official government support from a church
It is considered the longest non-technical, non-obscure word in English.

Lake Chargoggagoggmanchauggagoggchaubunagungamaugg
This lake in Massachusetts is the longest place name in the United States.

Floccinaucinihilipilification
Meaning: the action or habit of estimating something as worthless

LITTLE BIG STATE

The official name of Rhode Island is "The State of Rhode Island and Providence Plantations." That makes it the smallest state with the biggest name!

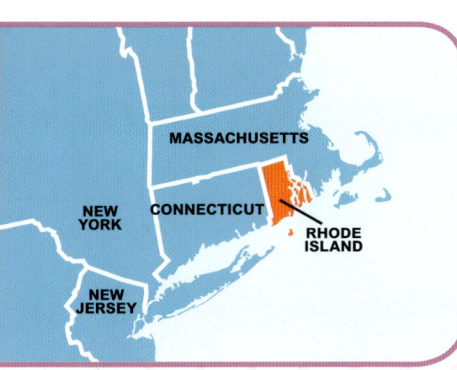

COMPOUND WORDS

The technical chemical name for the protein titin is 189,819 letters long. It is so long that it takes more than three hours to say the whole name! Here's just part of it.

Methionylalanylthreonylserylarginylglycylalanylserylarginylcysteinylprolylarginylaspartylisoleucylalanylasparaginylvalylmethionylglutaminylarginylleucylglutaminylaspartylglutamylglutaminylglutamylisoleucylvalylglutaminyllysylarginylthreonylphenylalanylthreonyllysyltryptophylisoleucylasparaginylserylhistidylleucylalanyllysylarginyllysylprolylprolylmethionylvalylvalylaspartylaspartylleucylphenylalanylglutamylaspartylmethionyllysylaspartylglycylvalyllysylleucylleucylalanylleucylleucylglutamylvalylleucylserylglycylglutaminyllysylleucylprolylcysteinylglutamylglutaminylglycylarginylarginylmethionyllysylarginylisoleucylhistidylalanylvalylalanylasparaginylisoleucylglycylthreonylalanylleucyllysylphenylalanylleucylglutamylglycylarginyllysylisoleucyllysylleucylvalylasparaginylisoleucylasparaginylserylthreonylaspartylisoleucylalanylaspartylglycylarginylprolylserylisoleucylvalylleucylglycylleucylmethionyltryptophylthreonylisoleucylisoleucylleucyltyrosylphenylalanylglutaminylisoleucylglutamylglutamylleucylthreonylserylasparaginylleucylprolylglutaminylleucylglutaminylserylleucylserylserylserylalanylserylserylvalylaspartylserylisoleucylvalylserylserylglutamylthreonylprolylserylprolylprolylserylysylarginyllysylvalylthreonylthreonyll

WORDS AND LANGUAGE

Nyctophobia
Fear of the dark

Terms of Terror
THE OFFICIAL NAMES FOR FEARS

Are you afraid of spiders? Speaking in public? Nearly everyone is afraid of something. But what is the term for it?

Here are the names of some common—and some very uncommon—fears.

BUTTON UP

Triskaidekaphobia is the fear of the number 13. This may seem silly, but it is so common that many buildings in the U.S. don't have a number 13 elevator button!

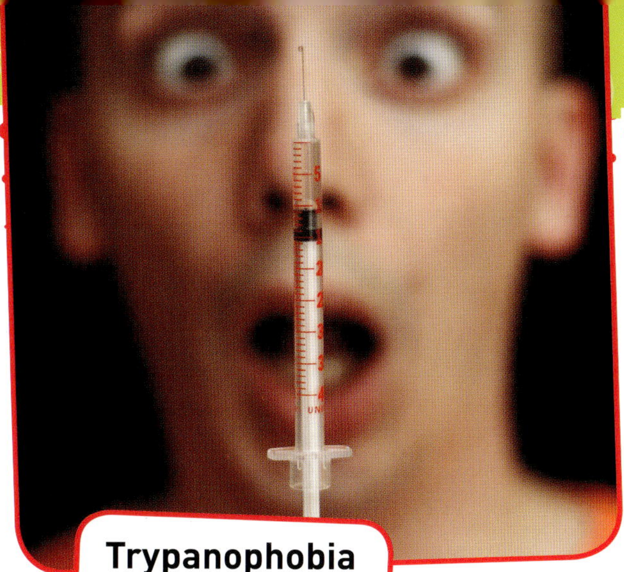

Trypanophobia
Fear of needles

Abibliophobia
Fear of running out of things to read

Arachnophobia
Fear of spiders

Glossophobia
Fear of speaking in public

Ophidiophobia
Fear of snakes

Pediophobia
Fear of dolls

Acrophobia
Fear of heights

161

WORDS AND LANGUAGE

Part of the Team

AWESOME NAMES FOR GROUPS OF ANIMALS AND HUMANS

When a **bunch** of the same animals get together, what do you call them? Here are some awesome names for groups of animals . . . and a few human groups, too.

ANIMALS

- A **clowder** of cats
- A **murder** of crows
- A **sloth** of bears
- A **swarm** of bees
- A **crash** of rhinoceroses
- A **romp** of otters
- An **army** of caterpillars
- A **herd** of cattle
- A **flock** of chickens
- A **bask** of crocodiles
- A **pack** of dogs
- A **school** of dolphins
- A **band** of gorillas
- A **troop** of monkeys
- A **scurry** of squirrels

162

A **flock** of sheep
A **cast** of hawks
A **bloat** of hippopotamuses
A **smack** of jellyfish
A **labor** of moles
A **barren** of mules
A **watch** of nightingales
A **rafter** of turkeys
A **pod** of whales
A **game** of swans
A **descent** of woodpeckers
A **zeal** of zebras
An **ostentation** of peacocks
A **business** of ferrets
A **colony** of rabbits
A **pride** of lions
A **colony** of bats

AND PEOPLE

A **blush** of boys
A **hastiness** of cooks
A **stalk** of foresters
A **faith** of merchants
A **superfluity** of nuns
A **pity** of prisoners

WORDS AND LANGUAGE

Cover Up!

SOME AMAZING FACTS ABOUT BOOKS AND READING

From comic books and novels to dictionaries, books are full of ideas, facts, and fun. Right now you're reading a page in an awesome book . . . about awesome books!

BOOK TREE-PORT

A library in Alnarp, Sweden, has a 217-volume collection of special wooden boxes made to look like books. Each "book" in the Wooden Library is dedicated to a specific tree; the covers are made from the wood of the tree and are decorated with its bark and mosses. Inside the box are dried leaves, seeds and other parts of the tree; also, a description of the tree can be found inside the spine. The collection was made in Germany in the 1800s.

HAVE BOOKS, WILL TRAVEL

England's M6 toll road is paved with 2,500,000 books, ground up and mixed into the materials to keep the surface from cracking.

FUN FACTS!

- There are an estimated 130 million different books in existence. About two million new books are published each year.
- The Japanese word *tsundoku* means "buying a load of books and then not getting around to reading them."
- Bibliosmia is the term for "enjoying the smell of old books."
- *The Adventures of Tom Sawyer* is said to be the first novel to be written using a typewriter.
- Printed in 1933, *Famous Funnies: A Carnival of Comics* is widely considered to be the first modern American comic book.
- In 2012, a team of 998 people in Sydney, Australia, set the record for the most people balancing books on their heads at the same place and time.
- *The Complete Miss Marple,* a collection of novels and short stories by Agatha Christie, is the thickest book ever published. It has 4,032 pages, its spine measures over a foot (0.3 meter), and it weighs over 17 pounds (7.7 kilograms).

HEAVY READING

Taken together, the Tripitaka tablets at the Kuthodaw Pagoda in Myanmar have been called the world's largest book. They are actually a collection of 729 carved stone tablets. Each one is 5 feet (1.5 meters) tall and housed in its own small structure.

FOOD

Hot, Hot, Hot!

MEASURING THE WORLD'S HOTTEST PEPPERS

What makes a chili so hot? Most hot peppers contain a molecule called capsaicin that reacts with sensors in the mouth and throat.

In 1912, a scientist named Wilbur Scoville invented a method to measure the hotness of peppers. Today, peppers are rated using the Scoville Heat Index and are measured in Scoville Heat Units (SHUs).

HELP! I JUST ATE A GHOST PEPPER! WHAT DO I DO?

If you take a bite of a pepper that's too spicy, DON'T drink water! Water will just spread the chili's hot ingredients around your mouth. Instead, these things can help you put out the fire:

- Milk or cheese
- Lemon juice
- Tomato juice
- Pasta or bread

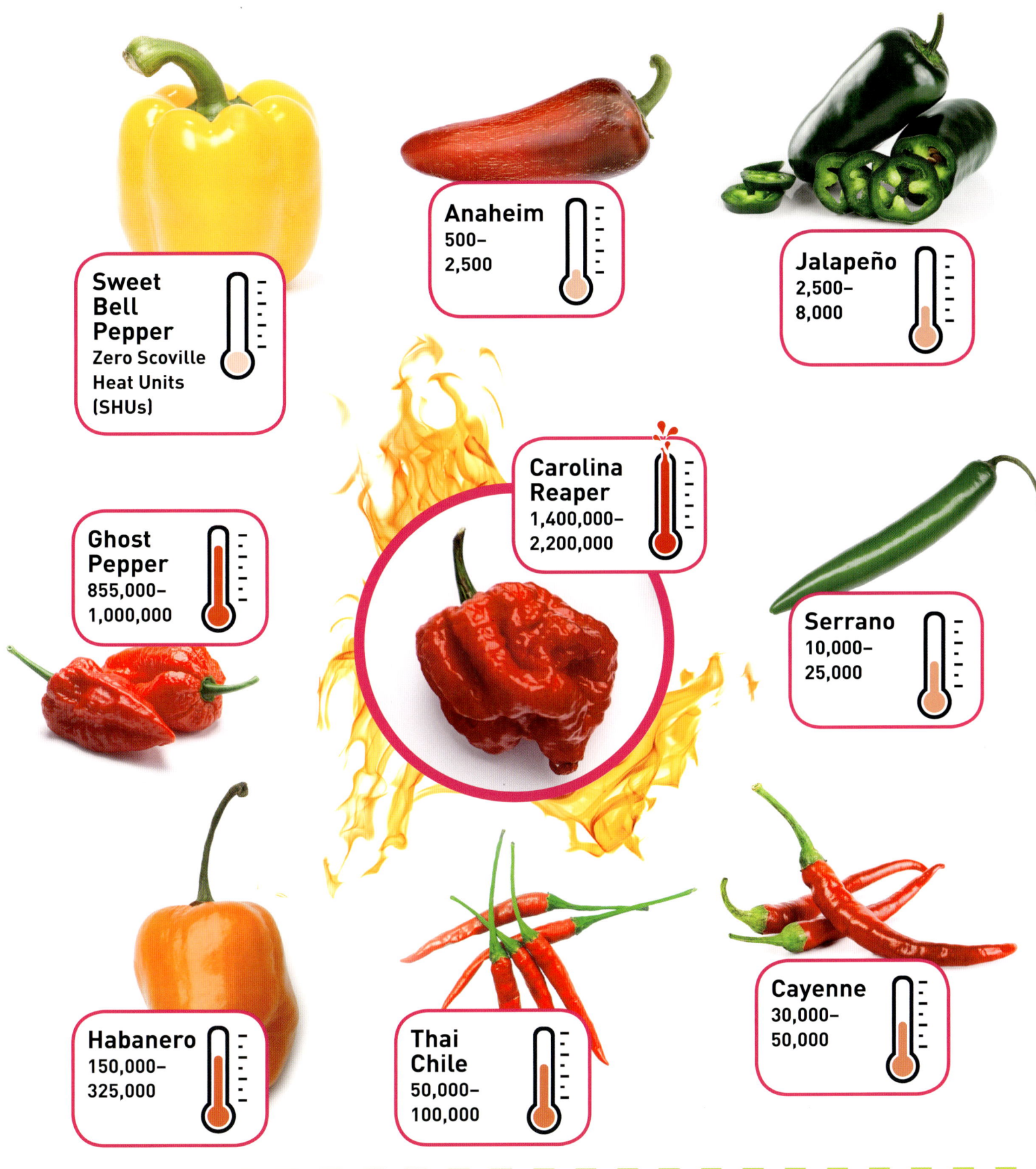

FOOD

Snack Time!

Between meals or late at night. Healthful or loaded with sugar and fat. Here are some amazing facts about all kinds of snacks.

CHIPS, SWEETS, AND TASTY TREATS

In 1974, Wrigley's chewing gum became the first product to have its **bar code** scanned at a checkout counter. It was a 10-pack package of Juicy Fruit®.

Beans from pacay pods are a popular snack in Peru dating back to the time of the Incas.

Buy Me Some Peanuts and Cracker Jack

It has been estimated that since 1940, when crowds started singing "Take Me Out to the Ball Game" at Major League Baseball games, Cracker Jack® has received more than $588 million worth of free advertising.

According to legend, Italian monks invented **pretzels** in 610 CE. They folded strips of dough to make it look like their young students praying.

In Peru, archaeologists have found evidence of **popcorn** from about 6,700 years ago!

When you chew gum, you burn about 11 **calories** per hour.

Stuffed pastries or **dumplings** are popular in Egypt, Zanzibar, China, and many other countries. A well-known Indian stuffed snack is the samosa.

FOOD

Chocolate syrup is the world's most popular ice cream topping.

DID YOU KNOW?

According to some surveys, ice cream is America's favorite dessert. It's estimated that Americans eat nearly 5 gallons (19 liters) of ice cream per person per year. Vanilla is the best-selling flavor.

POPSICLE FUN FACTS!

- Over two billion Popsicle® ice pops are sold every year. Cherry is the most popular flavor.
- Frank Epperson was only 11 years old when he invented the ice pop in 1905. He called his frozen treat "Epsicles." Years later, his children, who called him Pop, convinced him to change the name to "Popsicles."

Nine percent of all the **milk** produced in the U.S. is turned into ice cream.

America's first **ice cream parlor** opened in New York City in the late 1700s.

Employees who work for **Ben & Jerry's®** are allowed to bring home three pints of ice cream every day.

It takes 3 gallons (11 liters) of milk to make 1 gallon (3.8 liters) of **ice cream**.

You Scream, I Scream

ICE CREAM AND OTHER FROZEN TREATS

Eighty-seven percent of Americans have ice cream or other frozen treats in their freezer. Here's the scoop on our favorite chilly sweets.

GREAT MOMENTS IN ICE CREAM

There is a lot of controversy over who really invented the ice cream cone. According to one popular story, an ice cream vendor at the 1904 World's Fair in St. Louis ran out of bowls. A neighboring waffle vendor named Ernest Hamwi rolled a waffle into the shape of a cone for people to hold their ice cream. Even if this isn't the true story behind the cone, the fair made the treat famous, and the world has never been the same!

FOOD

DID YOU KNOW?

Animal crackers have been around since the 1800s. In 1902, the popular Barnum's Animals® brand was introduced. Originally designed to be a Christmas novelty, the boxes had a string handle so that people could hang them from their Christmas trees.

How Sweet It Is!

FACTS ABOUT CANDY AND COOKIES

Be sure to brush your teeth when you're done reading these sweet facts!

SEE THE LIGHT

Hard sugar candies actually spark a little bit when crushed. That's because the sugar molecules break apart. This phenomenon is called triboluminescence. Wintergreen candy does it more than other candies because wintergreen oil is fluorescent, meaning it absorbs light that you can't see and gives off visible light.

Marshmallows were originally made from the root of a plant called mallow.

The two Ms in **M&M® brand** candies stand for Forrest Mars Sr. and Bruce Murrie, the candy company's two owners.

The **Snickers®** candy bar was named after a horse belonging to Frank Mars, the Mars candy company's founder.

Chocolate was once used as currency. The ancient Maya and the Aztecs used the cocoa bean as a system of money.

Women are more likely than men to pull apart their **Oreo®** cookies before eating them.

FOOD

Fresh!

FRESHLY PICKED FACTS ABOUT FRUITS AND VEGETABLES

Just to be clear, if it's from a plant *and* it has seeds, it's a fruit. If it doesn't have seeds, it's a vegetable. Tomatoes, cucumbers, and chili peppers are fruits. Spinach is a vegetable.

The white "seeds" of a strawberry are not really seeds. These little bumps are actually individual fruits called **achenes**, each with a seed inside.

FUN FACTS!

- Apples are about 25% air. That's why they float.
- Archaeologists have found evidence that humans have been eating apples since at least 6500 BCE.
- It takes about 36 apples to create 1 gallon (3.7 liters) of apple cider.
- The world's longest unbroken apple peel was created in 1976. It was 172 feet 4 inches (52 m 10 cm) long. The woman who peeled it was 16 years old at the time. She had grown up working on her family's apple orchard and nursery.
- Orchards in the U.S. grow 2,500 different types of apples. Around the world, 7,500 varieties of apples are grown.

DID YOU KNOW?

Apples, potatoes, and onions all taste the same when our sense of smell is obstructed. If you close your eyes and pinch your nose, you might not be able to tell them apart. Try it!

Green-skinned **Granny Smith apples** are named after an Australian woman, Maria Ann "Granny" Smith. She cultivated the apples in 1868.

Carrots were originally purple. In the 1600s, people began to cultivate them in different colors.

A single tree planted in the late 1920s is linked to 95 percent of all **California avocados**.

Raisins are dried grapes. **Prunes** are dried plums.

The **pineapple** originated in South America. They weren't grown in Hawaii until the 1800s.

FOOD

Griddle Me This

FACTS ABOUT **BREAKFAST**

Sometime in the 1400s, the word "breakfast" entered the written English language. Before that, people sometimes used the Old English word *morgenmete*, meaning "morning meal." No matter what you call it, the first food of the day is important—and tasty!

Recipes for **pancakes** have been found in cookbooks from as far back as the 1500s.

In 2015, a group of 418 people at the Sheraton Langfang Chaobai River Hotel in Langfang, Hebei, China, set the record for eating **breakfast in bed**. They enjoyed the hotel's breakfast on 225 beds.

FUN **FACT!**

The record for running a marathon while continuously **flipping a pancake** in a frying pan? Three hours, two minutes, and 27 seconds.

Toast with chocolate sprinkles is the most popular breakfast in the Netherlands. It's called **hagelslag**, which means "hailstorm."

National Waffle Day is on August 24, because the first U.S. patent for a waffle iron was awarded that day in 1869.

The average person sits down to **breakfast** at 7:31 a.m. during the week and 8:28 a.m. on the weekend.

The earliest known breakfast food was a kind of **porridge**. Early humans made it by grinding grains with a stone.

FOOD

Order Up!

AWESOME FACTS ABOUT LUNCH AND DINNER

Digest these fascinating food facts!

In many countries, including Portugal and Egypt, asking for **salt** or **pepper** is considered a huge insult to the chef.

ONE SMALL BITE FOR MANKIND

The *Apollo 11* astronauts ate the very first meal on the Moon. It consisted of bacon squares, peaches, sugar cookie cubes, pineapple-grapefruit drink, and coffee.

There are approximately 350 different **pasta** shapes around the world.

French fries may not actually have been invented in France. Some claim they came from Belgium.

Seventy percent of all the **spices** in the world come from one country—India!

The first food intentionally microwaved was **popcorn**. Next, the inventor tried to microwave an egg—and it exploded.

HAVE YOU HERD?

A single fast-food hamburger can contain meat from 100 different cows!

According to the World **Instant Noodles** Association, China consumed more than 46 billion packets of ramen in 2013.

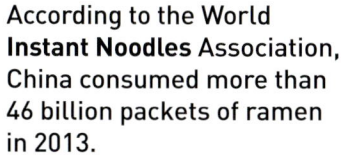

Herring is the most widely eaten fish in the world.

It's been estimated that Americans eat 50 billion **hamburgers** each year. That's enough to wrap around the equator more than 32 times.

FOOD

DID YOU KNOW?

Herbs are just the leaves of plants. Spices can be any part of a plant except the leaves.

Season's Greetings

FLAVORS AND SPICES

Spices, herbs, and sugars preserve and add flavor to our food. Flavor your brain with some flavorful facts.

Indonesia and Madagascar rank numbers 1 and 2 in world **vanilla** production.

FOREVER SWEET

If honey is kept in a sealed container, it will never go bad. Archaeologists in Egypt have found 3,000-year-old honey. It was still safe to eat!

SMELLED BETTER, DIDN'T CURE

When there were plagues of disease in medieval Europe, doctors often wore masks with long beaks filled with items like mint leaves, rose petals, and cloves. They believed that bad-smelling air caused disease. (The beaks didn't help at all.)

Banana trees are actually giant herbs. Their "trunks" are made of leaves, not wood.

Ancient Greeks and Romans are said to have believed that **basil** grew better if you cursed and shouted while sowing the seeds.

Pepper is the best-selling spice in the world.

PRICEY SPICE

Saffron is the most expensive spice. It can cost several thousand dollars a pound. That's because it takes 75,000 flowers to produce a pound (454 grams) of the spice.

FOOD

Secret Ingredients

WHAT'S HIDDEN IN YOUR FAVORITE FOODS?

It's time we had a little talk about some of the stuff that might be in your food. Warning: You might not want to eat anything ever again!

Ice cream often contains **seaweed**. It acts as a thickening agent.

Castoreum, a fluid beavers secrete to mark territory, was first used as a food additive in the early 20th century. Rarely used now, it is still considered a "natural flavor" by the U.S. Food and Drug Administration.

Soft chewing gum often contains **lanolin**, which is oil from sheep's wool.

Mass-produced bread and rolls often contain L-cysteine, made from **duck feathers**.

Gelatin is made by boiling down animal bones, skin, and connective tissue. Often, one of the ingredients in gelatin is **pig skin**.

Maraschino cherries, along with many jams, cakes, and tomato products, contain red dye made from **cochineal beetles**.

Grated Parmesan cheese sometimes contains **cellulose** from trees to keep it from clumping.

FOOD

Global Gourmets
SPECIALTY FOODS FROM AROUND THE WORLD

If you've been eating a lot of the same old things lately, maybe it's time for something totally different. These dishes might seem a bit strange at first, but they're loaded with vitamins and protein. Are you brave enough to try a bite?

Cambodia
Fried spiders

Turkey
Kelle paça—stewed sheep's feet and head

South Korea
Boiled silkworm pupae

Scotland
Haggis—sheep's heart, liver, and lungs, cooked inside the stomach

France
Escargots—snails in a wine, garlic, and butter sauce

Australia
Witchetty grubs

FOOD

Table Talk

HOW DID FOODS GET THEIR NAMES?

From foreign languages to famous animals, all kinds of names have made it to our tables.

FAKE CAKE?

"German chocolate cake" is actually American! German's Sweet Chocolate, a baking chocolate named after the inventor Sam German, was used to make a cake called German's Sweet Chocolate Cake. Later, the name was shortened, confusing most people about its origins.

The word **waffle** might have come from the Old German word *wabo*, which means "honeycomb."

In Italian, **linguine** means "little tongues."

FINGER FOOD

The sandwich is named after John Montagu, 4th Earl of Sandwich, an English noble born in 1718. According to legend, he asked the kitchen staff to put meat between two slices of bread so he could eat while playing cards.

Ketchup comes from the southeastern Chinese word *kê-tsiap*, which was a condiment made of fish brine. First encountered by European sailors in the 1600s, similar dark, savory sauces soon became popular in Europe and North America. People began adding tomatoes to their recipes in the early 1800s, and ketchup took over tables across the U.S.

Cola is named for the cola (or kola) nut tree, found in western Africa. Colas like Coke and Pepsi originally contained the fruit from that tree.

Butter comes from the ancient Greek word *bouturon*, meaning "cow cheese."

The man who claims to have invented the modern **lollipop**—in 1908 in Connecticut—said he named it after a famous racehorse at the time: Lolly Pop.

   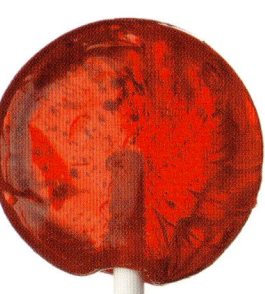 

187

TOYS, GAMES, AND SPORTS

Let's Play!

ORIGINS OF FAVORITE TOYS

Where did some of your favorite playthings come from? How did they get their names? Here are some awesome facts about toys.

The **Frisbee®** got its start when people began tossing around the tin plates that came with pies from the Frisbie Pie Company.

The inventor of **K'Nex®** came up with the idea for the toy while playing with drinking straws at a wedding.

DID YOU KNOW?

There is evidence that yo-yos were popular toys in ancient Greece, but some historians think they were first invented in China. Centuries later, spinning toys on strings could still be found all over Asia and Europe, where they went by names like "quiz" and "bandalore." Introducing the modern version to the United States in 1928, a Filipino immigrant called the toy a "yo-yo" after the name used in his home country.

More than 7 billion **Hot Wheels**® and **Matchbox**® cars have been made!

Over 350 million **Rubik's**® **Cube** have been sold worldwide!

Play-Doh® was originally created in the 1930s as a way to clean wallpaper.

The name **Crayola**® comes from the combination of the French words *craie* (chalk) and *oléagineuse* (oily).

TOYS, GAMES, AND SPORTS

Bits and Pieces

CARDS, PUZZLES, AND **BOARD GAMES**

Here are some facts about the origins of games and puzzles.

A British mapmaker named John Spilsbury made the first **jigsaw puzzle** around 1766. He cut up maps to help children learn geography. Puzzles continued to be used mainly as educational tools for decades before becoming toys.

Games similar to **backgammon** were played as far back as 5,000 years ago. The Roman emperor Claudius played a game called tabula, an early version of backgammon.

Charles Darrow became the first millionaire game designer when he sold the game **Monopoly** to Parker Brothers in the 1930s. A woman named Elizabeth Magie had patented a similar game called The Landlord's Game in 1904, though.

PRINT A MINT

Each year, Hasbro prints more **Monopoly money** than the United States Mint produces in real currency.

Checkers might have its roots in ancient Egypt. Checkers-like games have been found from as early as 1400 BCE.

Card games have their origins in China between 600 and 900 CE. Historians think they started when people were trading and shuffling paper money.

TOYS, GAMES, AND SPORTS

Stuffed!
THE STORIES BEHIND DOLLS AND STUFFED ANIMALS

Teddy Roosevelt

Teddy Bear

Bobblehead Doll

Dolls are some of the earliest known toys. Here are some awesome facts about dolls and our stuffed fuzzy friends.

- Dolls have been found in Egyptian tombs from as far back as 2000 BCE.
- Rag dolls from ancient Rome date back to 300 BCE.
- A German company named Steiff produced the first brand of stuffed animals in 1880.
- The first patented stuffed toy was Peter Rabbit, based on the character from stories by Beatrix Potter.
- The teddy bear was named after U.S. President Theodore "Teddy" Roosevelt, in honor of a popular tale at the time: Roosevelt went hunting and refused to shoot a cornered and tied-up black bear.
- Ruth Handler invented the Barbie® doll in 1959. She named the doll after her daughter, Barbara. (Two years later, she named the Ken doll after her son.)
- The first Western mention of a bobblehead doll is from the 1842 story "The Overcoat" by the Russian writer Nikolai Gogol. It mentions a character whose collar makes his neck look long, like the "necks of plaster cats which wag their heads."

Barbie®

BEARS IN SPACE

In 1995, a teddy bear named Magellan T. Bear flew with astronauts aboard NASA's Space Shuttle *Discovery*.

TOYS, GAMES, AND SPORTS

Blocked!

THE TRUTH ABOUT CONSTRUCTION TOYS

From wooden blocks to plastic bricks, construction toys let kids stack and build.

Lincoln Logs®, the miniature logs with notches in them, were named after U.S. President Abraham Lincoln, who lived in a log cabin for part of his childhood.

FEW BRICKS, MANY OPTIONS

Six eight-stud **Lego®** bricks can be combined into 915,103,765 different configurations.

194

EARLY READERS

One of the first known references to **alphabet blocks** came in 1693. The philosopher John Locke wrote that dice toys should have letters on them "to teach children the alphabet by playing."

Used by kids around the world, **unit blocks**—also known as standard unit or kindergarten blocks—are wooden blocks in basic shapes.

TOYS, GAMES, AND SPORTS

Sport Rules!
IT'S HOW YOU PLAY THE GAME

A sport is a physical activity in which individuals or teams compete against each other under a set of rules.

Here are some basics of some of the most popular sports around.

FUN FACT!

A marathon is a 26.2 mile (42.2-kilometer) race. The name and distance were chosen because of the legend of the Greek soldier who is said to have run over 25 miles (40.2 kilometers) to announce that Greece had won a battle at the town of Marathon.

DID YOU KNOW?

The sport of soccer was originally called "association football" when the rules were officially set in England in the 1860s. People started calling the players "assoc-ers." This became shortened and changed to "soccers" or "soccer football." Most of the world calls it football, though.

Soccer
Soccer is the most popular sport on the planet. Two teams of 11 players each try to get a ball into the other team's net using anything except their hands.

Tennis
One on one (singles) or two on two (doubles), players use rackets to hit a ball over a net.

Basketball
Two teams of five players pass, throw, roll, or dribble a ball, scoring points by tossing it into the other team's net.

Baseball
Players use a bat to hit a ball, giving them time to run around three bases and score at home plate.

Football
Teams pass or carry a ball, fighting to move it over the other side's goal line.

Golf
Players use clubs to hit balls long distances, trying to sink them into holes with as few hits as possible.

Volleyball
Using just their hands, teams hit a ball back and forth over a high net. If the ball touches the ground on one side, the other team scores.

Polo
Two teams of players on horseback use sticks to hit a ball into their opponents' net.

Hockey
While skating on ice, two teams use sticks to knock a puck into their opponents' net.

Curling
Teams slide stones down lanes of ice. Scraping and sweeping a pathway, they steer the stone toward the bull's-eye.

Lacrosse
Teams catch, throw, and carry a ball in sticks fitted with nets. Unlike many field sports, lacrosse players can move behind the goal area.

TOYS, GAMES, AND SPORTS

The largest game of **dodgeball** had 6,084 players.

The record for the farthest run on a **treadmill** in 24 hours is 162.29 miles (261.18 kilometers).

The longest ride by a dog on a **surfboard** lasted 351.7 feet (107.2 meters).

Goofy Greatness
AWESOME AND STRANGE SPORTS RECORDS

The record for **smashing watermelons** with a fist: 70 melons in one minute!

We salute the brave, bold, and totally zany sports record-breakers.

FUN FACTS!

- The fastest marathoner in a fruit costume—a banana—finished in 2 hours, 47 minutes, and 41 seconds.
- The fastest marathoner wearing a vegetable costume—a carrot—finished in 2 hours, 59 minutes, and 33 seconds.

The most **uneven score** in an international ice hockey game: 82–0.

The largest **rock-paper-scissors** game had 2,950 players competing at the same time.

ALL THAT GLITTERS

The 1912 Olympic Games were the last time the gold medals were solid gold. Since then, the medals have been made of silver with gold plating.

TOYS, GAMES, AND SPORTS

Whack!
PROJECTILES OF THE GAMES

Here are some interesting facts about the objects athletes roll, hit, pass, and throw.

A regulation **bowling ball** can weigh up to 16 pounds (7.25 kilograms).

The outside of a **baseball** is leather. The inside is wool string wrapped around a rubber-coated cork.

HOW LONG IS IT?

Tennis racket	27–29 in (69–74 cm)
Field-hockey stick	32–36 in (81–91 cm)
Golf club	36–45 in (91–114 cm)
Cricket bat	38 in (97 cm)
Baseball bat	32–42 in (81–107 cm)
Lacrosse stick	40–72 in (102–183 cm)
Hockey stick	52–60 in (132–152 cm)

The first rubber **hockey pucks** were made by slicing rubber balls.

FUN FACT!

A badminton shuttle, which is also called a **shuttlecock**, was traditionally made using 16 goose feathers.

When hit by a pro, a **golf ball** can reach speeds of more than 200 miles (321 kilometers) per hour.

According to regulations, a **table tennis** ball must bounce 9–10 inches (24–26 centimeters) when dropped from a height of 12 inches (30.5 centimeters).

A **soccer** ball has 32 panels: 20 hexagons and 12 pentagons.

The condition of a **cricket** ball is very important. If the ball wears out during a match, the umpire will replace it.

TOYS, GAMES, AND SPORTS

Rule Breakers

SOME LESSER-KNOWN SPORTS REGULATIONS

You probably know basketball players must dribble the ball as they run down the court, or that when baseball players get three strikes, they're out. But do you know about these unusual rules? Brush up on them—or pay the price!

DID YOU KNOW?

In U.S. college **volleyball**, it is against the rules for both sides to wear very similar uniforms. If that happens, the game official decides who has to change.

If you don't sign your scorecard in **golf**, you can be disqualified from playing.

In **water polo**, it is illegal to splash water in an opponent's face.

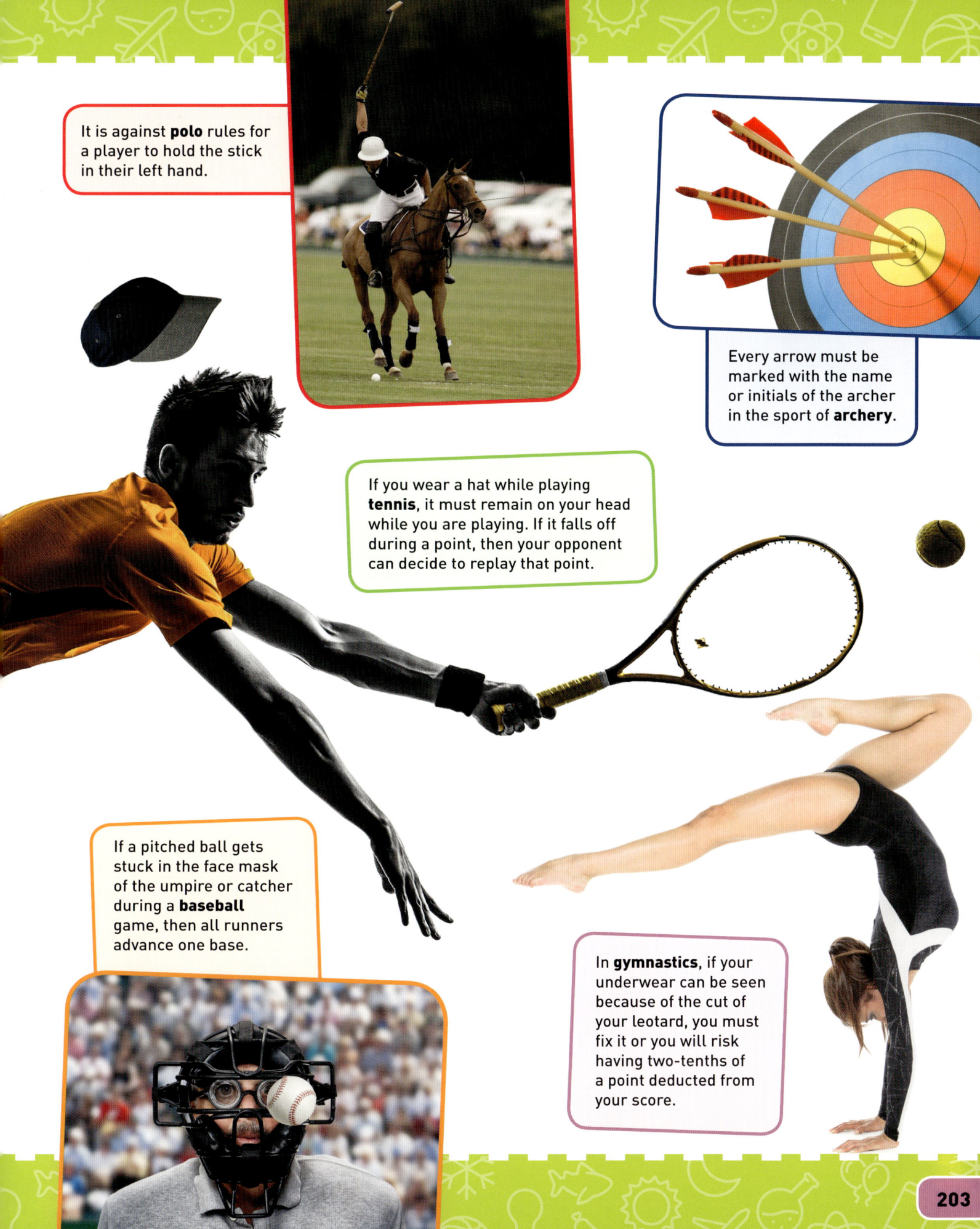

TOYS, GAMES, AND SPORTS

WILD AND WACKY COMPETITIONS

Weird World of Sports

Are soccer and basketball not unusual enough for you? Here are some of the strangest sports ever played.

At lumberjack competitions in Canada, the U.S., and the U.K., players compete in **axe throwing** by hurling the tool at targets.

In the sport of **chessboxing**, competitors alternate between five rounds of boxing and six rounds of chess. This sport is played in Germany, the U.K., India, and Russia.

Racers use giant carved-out pumpkins as kayaks in a **pumpkin regatta**.

Toe wrestling is like arm wrestling, but players lock toes and try to pin their opponent's foot. You can toe wrestle in the U.K. and Canada.

In Wales, Australia, Ireland, and Sweden, players race through water-filled trenches carved into peat bogs. In the sport of **bog snorkeling**, you must use flipper power—it's illegal to do traditional swimming strokes.

Soccer played on bicycles is known as **cycle ball**, or "radball," and it is played in Austria, Belgium, the Czech Republic, Denmark, France, Germany, Japan, Russia, and Switzerland.

DID YOU KNOW?

Growing in popularity since it was invented in 2004, **bossaball** combines elements of soccer, volleyball, and gymnastics. You can use any part of your body to hit the ball to your opponent's side of the net. And it's played on an inflatable court with trampolines!

COMPARISONS

What Are the Odds?

CHANCES IN GAMES... AND A WHOLE LOT MORE

If you flip a coin, the odds are 1 in 2 that you'll get heads. Your odds of rolling a 12 with two dice are 1 in 36. Probability is at play everywhere. Here are some odds that experts have figured out for different events.

ZAPPED!

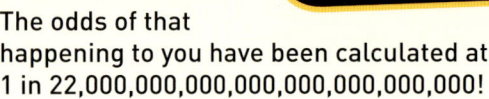

Forest ranger Roy Sullivan was struck by lightning seven times over the course of his life. The odds of that happening to you have been calculated at 1 in 22,000,000,000,000,000,000,000,000,000!

Tossing a coin and getting heads three times in a row: **1 in 8**

A baby being born with teeth:
1 in 2,000–3,000

Dying from a shark attack:
1 in 3,748,067

An NFL kickoff getting returned for a touchdown:
1 in 270

Finding a four-leaf clover:
1 in 10,000

Becoming a pro athlete:
1 in 22,000

A meteorite landing on your house on any given day:
1 in 2,196,267,379,587

Drawing five cards from a deck and getting a pair:
1 in 2.36

COMPARISONS

Up in the Air

HOW FAST AND HIGH ARE THINGS THAT FLY?

Up in the sky, things go fast and slow, low and high. Compare the speeds and altitudes of people, animals, and machines.

In 2012, **skydiver** Felix Baumgartner jumped from a balloon 24.5 miles (39.4 kilometers) above the Earth. He reached a speed of 833 miles (1,342.8 kilometers) per hour before opening his parachute.

ALTITUDE ADJUSTMENT

- Mosquitoes typically fly at heights of less than 25 ft (8 m).
- A mako shark can jump up to 30 ft (9 m) out of the water.
- Hot-air balloons typically cruise at 1,000 to 3,000 ft (305 to 914 m).
- A helium-filled balloon can reach a height of 29,537 ft (9,000 m), before it pops.
- An Andean condor can soar up to 15,000 ft (4572 m).
- Commercial airliners typically cruise at 36,000 ft (10,973 m)
- The record altitude for a weather balloon is 32.9 mi (52.9 km).

Party Balloons | Andean Condor | Weather Balloon

A **Boeing 747** can cruise at a speed of 650 miles (1,046 kilometers) per hour.

The **SR-71 Blackbird,** the fastest manned airplane, reached a speed of 2,193 miles (3,529 kilometers) per hour.

The **International Space Station** orbits Earth at a speed of 17,500 miles (28,164 kilometers) per hour.

The top speed of most **helicopters** is between 130 and 160 miles (209 and 257 kilometers) per hour.

The top speed of a **blimp** is about 70 miles (113 kilometers) per hour.

The Wright brothers' first plane, the **Wright Flyer,** flew at a speed of 30 miles (48 kilometers) per hour.

The top speed of a **racing pigeon** is 92.5 miles (149 kilometers) per hour.

COMPARISONS

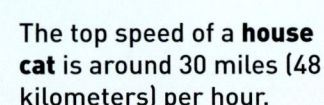

The top speed of a **house cat** is around 30 miles (48 kilometers) per hour.

The average speed of most **cyclists** is around 10 miles (16 kilometers) per hour.

The top speed for most **racing cyclists** is about 25 miles (40 kilometers) per hour.

The **average car** has a top speed of about 100 to 120 miles (161 to 193 kilometers) per hour.

On average, people **walk** at a speed of 3.1 miles (5 kilometers) per hour.

The fastest **human** speed was achieved by Usain Bolt, who ran at a speed of nearly 28 miles (45 kilometers) per hour.

The top speed of a **snail** is 0.03 miles (0.05 kilometers) per hour.

Hit the Road
COMPARING SPEEDS, FROM CRAWLING TO FLYING

Some things are built for speed, and some are not. How do some animals and machines compare when they hit the road?

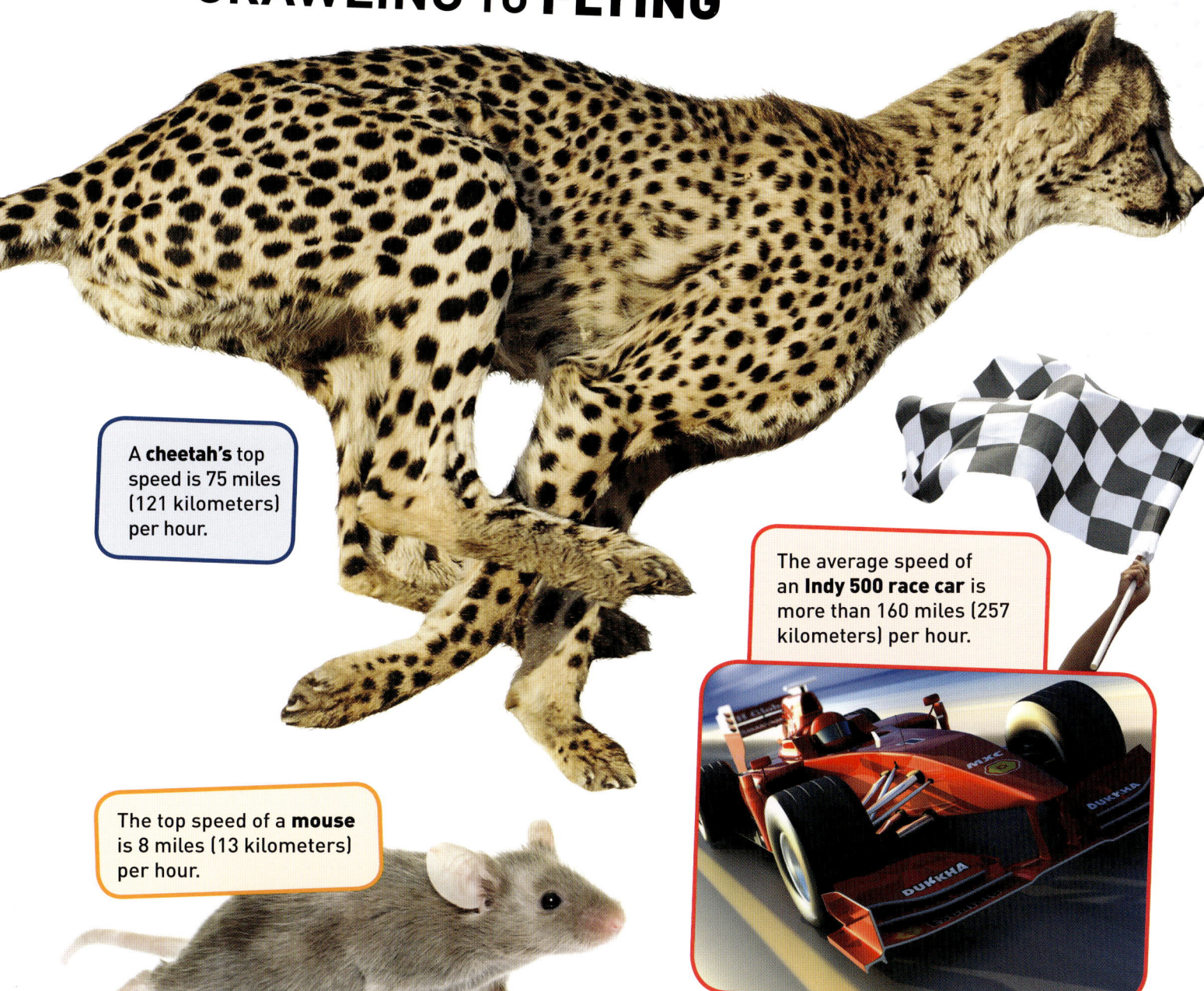

A **cheetah's** top speed is 75 miles (121 kilometers) per hour.

The average speed of an **Indy 500 race car** is more than 160 miles (257 kilometers) per hour.

The top speed of a **mouse** is 8 miles (13 kilometers) per hour.

COMPARISONS

TIME FLIES

It took just 66 years from the Wright brothers' first flight (1903) to the first astronauts landing on the Moon (1969).

Earth is about 4.5 billion years old.

CLOSE TO THE REX

Stegosaurus lived 150 million years ago. *Tyrannosaurus rex* lived 65 million years ago. That means the monster carnivore lived closer to you!

FUN FACTS!

- The universe is 13.8 billion years old.
- Life began on Earth about 3.8 billion years ago.
- The first anatomically modern humans appeared around 200,000 years ago.
- Humans invented agriculture 15,000 to 10,000 years ago.
- The first alphabet was developed about 4,000 years ago.
- The first programmable computer was built in 1938.
- The World Wide Web started in 1989—only about 30 years ago.

Growing Up

COMPARING THE AGE OF THINGS

As time flows forward, everything ages.

The first practical **steam engine** was invented in 1712 (about 300 years ago).

The first steam-powered passenger **elevator** was installed in 1857.

MODERN QUEEN?

Cleopatra lived closer to your lifetime than to the days when the Great Pyramid was being built! The Great Pyramid was built around 2500 BCE. Cleopatra lived from around 69 BCE to 30 BCE. You are living almost 500 years closer to her.

COMPARISONS

Is It Hot in Here?
COMPARING TEMPERATURES

Explore these **extreme temperatures** to find out what's hot and what's not.

The temperature of **molten lava** can vary between 1,300 and 2,200 degrees Fahrenheit (700 and 1,200 degrees Celsius).

The surface temperature of **the Sun** is about 10,000 degrees Fahrenheit (5,538 degrees Celsius), although it can get even hotter.

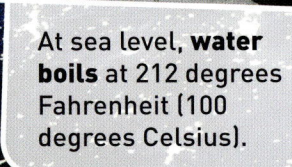

At sea level, **water boils** at 212 degrees Fahrenheit (100 degrees Celsius).

The average normal **human body** temperature is 98.6 degrees Fahrenheit (37 degrees Celsius).

The temperature of **outer space** is -455 degrees Fahrenheit (-271 degrees Celsius).

The temperature of **Earth's core** gets up to about 10,800 degrees Fahrenheit (6,000 degrees Celsius).

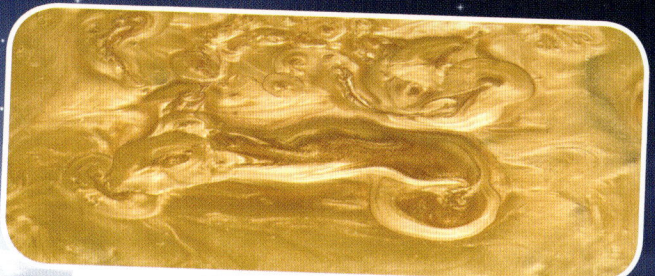

Gold melts at 1,948 degrees Fahrenheit (1,064 degrees Celsius).

The average surface temperature of **Venus** is 864 degrees Fahrenheit (462 degrees Celsius).

THERE'S NO PLACE LIKE HOME

- The hottest air temperature ever officially recorded on Earth was in Death Valley, California, in 1913: 134°F (56.7°C).
- The coldest air temperature ever officially recorded on Earth was in Antarctica in 1983: -128.6°F (-89.2°C).

Death Valley, California

Antarctica

215

COMPARISONS

Dare to Compare

SOME **MONUMENTAL** EQUIVALENTS

We took the time to do some incredible calculations. They're not really useful—but they're pretty awesome!

The Sun is as bright as 22 septillion LED light bulbs!

ROUND TRIP

If you ran once around **the equator**, it would be the same as running about 950 marathons.

A male **African elephant** can weigh as much as 300,000 mice!

DID YOU KNOW?

If you didn't stop, you could sing the song **"Happy Birthday to You"** approximately 4,000 to 6,000 times on your birthday.

A **blue whale** can weigh as much as 22 million goldfish!

The **Statue of Liberty** is as tall as 57 women, of average height, standing on top of one another.

217

Index

A
abibliophobia 161
Abstract Art 118
Abstract Expressionism 119
acrophobia 161
Adventures of Superman 131
aerial screw 87
Africa 180
age of dinosaurs 19
aglet 149
Airbus A380 86
airliner 208
airplane 87, 209
airship 88, 89
Aldabra giant tortoise 27
alphabet 151, 152, 212
alphabet blocks 195
ALS Association 135
ALS Ice Bucket Challenge 135
Altair 8800 93
Altamira Cave 115
American 28, 37, 77, 83, 103, 108, 109, 116, 127, 128, 137, 156, 158, 165, 171, 186
amusement park 138
amyotrophic lateral sclerosis (ALS) 135
Andalusian region 120
Andean condor 208
Andes Mountains 103, 110
Angkor Wat 103
animal crackers 172
Anji Bridge 80
Annual Duck Tape Festival 143
ant 40, 44, 67
Antarctica 101, 215
Antikythera mechanism 69
Apollo 11 178
apple 174
Apple 63, 75
Apple "Mothership" 75
arachnophobia 161
archery 203
archipelago 74
Archytas 96
Argentina 103, 107
Armstrong, Neil 127
army 151, 162
artifact 68
artificial intelligence 97
Ashoka Chakra 103
asteroid belt 11
asteroids 10, 11
astronauts landing on the Moon 212
Atlas moth 42
atmosphere 17
Australia 74, 103, 107, 165, 185, 205
avocado 175

B
Babbage, Charles 92
Babylon 111
backgammon 190
bacteria 46, 55, 65, 94
badminton 201
Bagger 293 77
Baghdad 111
Bailey 157
Baker 156
ballet dancer 137
balloons 88, 89, 208
ballroom dancing 137
banana 181
band 132, 162
bandalore 189
Barbie® doll 192, 193
Barcelona 75
barred spiral galaxy 7
Barrow, Alaska 112
baseball 197, 200, 202, 203
baseball cap 128
basil 181
bask 162
basketball 197, 202, 204
Bates, R.E. 122
Baumgartner, Felix 208
bdelloid rotifer 25
beach volleyball 202
beard 57
beavers 44
bee 40, 162
beehive 40
beekeeper suit 91
Belcher's sea snake 34
Bell Laboratories 67
Bengali 147
Berkeley Pit 79
Berners-Lee, Tim 63
bibliosmia 165
Bingham Canyon mine 79
bird 32
blimp 88, 89, 209
blink 47, 93
blobfish 31
blocks 194, 195
blood 48, 52, 53, 59, 103
blood cell 52
blood plasma 53
blood vessel 53, 59
blue-ringed octopus 35
blue whale 77, 217
board game 130, 131, 190
bobblehead doll 192
Boeing 747 209
bog snorkeling 205
Bolivia 107, 112
Bollywood 137
bomb suit 90
bomb technician 90
bone 50, 51, 66, 133, 183
bossaball 205
bowling 200
box jellyfish 34
brain 32, 41, 48, 58, 59, 121, 136, 180
bread 183
break-dancing 136
breakfast 176, 177
breath 47
bridge 80, 81, 127, 139
Brooklyn Excelsiors 128
bulldozer 76
bullet train 82
Buonarroti, Michelangelo 116
Burj Khalifa 72
burrow 44
butter 187

C
Caesar cipher 151
Caesar, Julius 151
cake 186
California 75, 77, 175, 215
Calment, Jeanne 27
Cambodia 103, 107, 185
Canada 107, 132, 204, 205
candy 172
Čapek, Karel 96
capsaicin 166
car 84, 85, 86, 138, 189, 210, 211
card games 191
cards 190
carnival 138
carnivorous plant 37
carousel 139
carrot 175
cartilage cell 48
cat 32, 210
cathedral termite 44
Cayley, George 86
cell 48, 49, 53, 54
center of the Earth 17
chance 206
Chandrayaan 1 20
Chauvet Cave 114
checkers 130, 191
cheese 166
cheetah 211
chef's hat 129
chess 130, 204
chessboxing 204
chewing gum 168, 183
Chicago 113, 116, 139
Chicago World's Fair 139
Chile 169
chimp 67
China 80, 82, 104, 107, 111, 147, 169, 189, 191
Chinese 62, 104, 132, 147, 156
Chinese Water Torture Cell act 132
chocolate 173
chromosphere 9
cinematograph 130
cipher 150, 151
circus 133
Civil War 28
Clark, Barney 66
Cleopatra 213
clowder 162
cocoa bean 173
code 150
Cold-water and ice rescue suit 91
collarbone 51
Colorado 81
comic book 164, 165
Commonwealth of Nations 103
computer 69, 92, 93, 109, 151, 212
concrete mixer 77
concrete paving rig 77
condensation 15
conga line 136
construction toy 194
contortionist 133
cookie 172
core 79, 215
corona 9
cowboy hat 128

cowboy's eyes 128
crab 33
crash 162
crater 10, 13, 18, 19
Crayola® 189
cricket 200
crust 17, 79
cryptography 150
Cubism 119
curling 197
cyclist 210

D

Da Vinci, Leonardo 87, 116, 117
Dada 119
Dalí, Salvadore 118
dance 136
dance marathon 136
Darrow, Charles 190
Dean, James 124
deathstalker scorpion 34
Death Valley 215
Debs, Eugene V. 109
democracy 108
devil ray 38
dinner 178
dirigible 88, 89
diver 34, 91
dodgeball 198
dolls 192
dolphin 67
Downrock 136
dragline 77
dragline excavator 77
dragonfly 42
Drosera 36
Dubai 72, 74
Duchamp, Marcel 119
dumplings 169

E

Earth 6, 9, 10, 11, 12, 14, 15, 17, 18, 19, 20, 21, 22, 27, 41, 43, 46, 78, 79, 140, 208, 209, 212, 215
Earth Day 140
eclipse 12
Egypt 66, 73, 107, 111, 130, 153, 169, 191
Egyptian mummies 145
Eiffel Tower 73
El Alto 112
electric car 84
electron 65

Electronic Numerical Integrator and Computer (ENIAC) 92
electron microscope 65
elephant 41, 44, 61, 216
elevator 160, 213
elliptical galaxy 7
Elvis 124
emoji 153
Empire State Building 72
engineering 62, 72, 80
England 69, 83, 105, 126, 165, 196
English 45, 133, 137, 146, 147, 154, 156, 159
enigma machine 151
entertainment 131
Epic of Gilgamesh, The 130
equator 179, 216
Euphrates 110
evaporation 15
excavation 78
excavator 77
Exosuit Atmospheric Diving System 91
Extravehicular Mobility Unit (EMU) 90
extreme environments 24
eye 32

F

fangtooth fish 30
fascinator hat 128
fastest human 60, 210
female egg cell 49
femur 51
Feringa, Ben 63
Fermi, Enrico 63
Ferris, Jr., George Washington 139
Ferris wheel 139
festival 142, 143
field hockey 200
fig tree 27
fire 66, 91
firefighter 91, 97
Fire Proximity Suit 91
first baseball team 128
first human in space 29
first microscope 64
Fitzgerald, Ella 121
flag 102, 103
flash mob 135
flea glasses 65
Fletcher 157
flock 81, 162, 163

Flyer III 86
flying car 86
flying fish 39
flying snake 39
flying squirrel 39
football 197, 201
Foote, Charles 77
Ford automotive assembly line 96
Ford, Henry 84
Fosset, Steve 88
France 73, 81, 85, 86, 88, 107, 115, 116, 129, 144, 178, 185, 205
Freezes 136
French 130, 141, 147, 153, 189
French fries 178
Frisbee™ 188
fruit 174
fusion 9
Futuro 70

G

Gabriel Green 109
galaxy 6, 7, 65
Galileo Galilei 62, 64
game 131, 154, 169, 206
gamma-ray telescope 65
gas giant 10
gasoline-powered automobile 84
gelatin 183
germ 94
giant barrel sponge 26
giant spider crab 31
giant tube worm 31
giant walking stick 43
giant weta 43
glabella 149
glass-bottom bridge 80
glider 86
gliding machine 86
Global Family Day 140
glossophobia 161
Gogol, Nikolai 192
gold 215
Goldilocks Zone, The 10
golf 197, 200, 201, 202
Goliath beetle 43
gorilla 67
Grand Prix of Endurance and Efficiency 85
Grant, Ulysses S. 108
grapes 175

Great Basin bristlecone pine tree 27
Great Pyramid 73, 213
Great Train Robbery, The 130
Greece 107, 124, 189, 196
Greeley, Horace 108
griffinfly 42
griffonage 149

H

hair 56, 57, 62, 124, 125, 183
hair follicle 57
Haiti 103, 107
Hal Saflieni Hypogeum 69
hamburger 179
Handler, Ruth 192
Hasbro 191
hat 128, 129, 203
heart 46, 52, 66, 136, 185
helicopter 87, 209
helium 11, 89
herbs 180, 181
herd 162
Hero 66
herring 179
hieroglyph 152
high-heeled shoe 126
Highline Meeting 143
high-speed train 82
highway 76, 77
Hindenburg 88
Hindi 137, 147
Hoba Meteorite 18
hockey 197, 200, 201
hole 78, 197
Holsinger Meteorite 19
home 67, 71, 74, 110, 131
honey 180
horseless carriage 84
hot-air balloon 87, 88, 208
hot peppers 166
Hot Wheels® 189
Houdini, Harry 132
house on a rock 70
Hubble Space Telescope 65
human 35, 47, 66, 67, 78, 90, 96, 129, 146, 174, 177, 212
human body 46, 47, 49, 53, 54, 60, 117, 214
human speed 210
hummingbird 41
humpback anglerfish 31
hydrosphere 14, 17
hydrothermal vents 25
Hypogeum 69

INDEX

I
I-90 77
I-95 77
ice 11, 14, 15, 91, 135, 170, 171, 182, 197, 199
ice cream 182
ice hockey 199
Impressionism 118
India 20, 103, 107, 113, 137, 144, 147, 179, 204
Indy 500 race car 211
inner core 17
insect 33, 37, 41, 42, 65
intelligent animals 45
International Chocolate Day 141
International Creativity and Innovation Day 140
International Lefthanders Day 141
International Literacy Day 141
International Space Station 109, 209
International Thank-You Day 140
International Volunteers Day 141
International Yoga Day 141
Interstate Highway System 77
Iran 81, 107
Iraq 105, 107, 111
Ireland 103, 107, 205
Iron Age 67
iron tool 67
irregular galaxy 7
Ismail al-Jazari 62
Italy 62, 107, 143

J
Jackson, Andrew 109
James Webb Space Telescope 65
Janssen, Hans 64
Janssen, Zacharias 64
Japan 81, 107, 205
Japanese maglev train 82
Japan's Akashi Kaikyo Bridge 81
jigsaw puzzle 190
Jobs, Steve 63
Jovian planet 10
Julian Acrobats 133
Julian, Rose 133
Jupiter 11, 20

K
Kandinsky, Wassily 118
Kansas Barbed Wire Museum 145
Katsushika Hokusai 117
Khaju Bridge 81
Kimberley diamond mine 79
kindergarten blocks 195
King Edward II 126
K'Nex® 188
Knickerbockers 128
Knievel, Evel 133
knife 67
Kola Superdeep Borehole 79
Kuwait City, Kuwait 113

L
lacrosse 197, 200
La Crosse 145
La Marche cave 129
Landlord's Game, The 190
language 137, 146, 147, 152, 154, 159
Lascaux Cave 115
last name 156
Lego™ 194
Le Mans 85
lemniscate 149
Liechtenstein 103, 107
Lincoln, Abraham 194
Lincoln Logs™ 194
Lindbergh, Charles 86
Lippershey, Hans 64
lithosphere 17
Locke, John 195
locomotive 83
logogram 153
lollipop 187
London's subway 83
Lone Ranger, The 131
long word 158
Lumière, Auguste 130
Lumière, Louis 130
lunar eclipse 12
lunch 178
Lunch Box Museum 145
lung 52, 185

M
Machu Picchu 110
Madagascar 180
Magellan T. Bear 193
Magie, Elizabeth 190
maglev train 82
magnet 82
magnetic fields 17
makeup 111
mako shark 208
mantle 17, 79
map 98, 99, 100, 101, 190
marathon 196
marathoner 199
Mariner 2 20
Mars 10, 11, 12, 20, 21, 96, 127, 173
marshmallows 173
Mars Pathfinder 20
Masonic cipher 150
Matchbox™ cars 189
Mayflower 29
McAdam, John 76
mechanical clock 62
medal 199
meganisoptera 42
Memphis 111
Mendoza 157
Mercator projection 101
Mercury 10, 20
Mesopotamia 105, 110, 111, 130
Messenger 20
Meteor Crater 18, 19
Met Life Tower 73
Mexico 103, 107, 145, 169
microrobot 97
microscope 64, 65
milk 166
Milky Way galaxy 6, 7
miner 78, 79
missions outside spacecraft 90
mobile device 93, 153
mobile phone 94, 95
mobula 38
Model T 84
molten lava 214
Monet, Claude 118
money 104
monkey cup 37
Monopoly 190, 191
Montgolfier brothers 88
monument 68
Moon 12, 13, 20, 21, 127, 178, 212
Morse code 151
mosquito 208
motion sickness 139
mouse 211
Mozart 121
Mumbai 137
Mummy Museum of Guanajuato 145
murder 162
muscle cell 48
museum 127, 144, 145
Myanmar 107, 165

N
names for fears 160
NASA 193
NASA's *Opportunity* 96
National Anthem Day 140
National Astronaut Day 141
National Bacon Day 141
National Best Friends Day 141
National Cereal Day 140
National Cheeseburger Day 141
National Cherry Popsicle Day 141
National Chess Day 141
National Clean Up Your Room Day 141
National Comic Book Day 141
National Cousins Day 141
National Crossword Puzzle Day 141
National Dictionary Day 141
National Dress Up Your Pet Day 140
National Earmuff Day 140, 141
National French Toast Day 141
National Fried Chicken Day 141
National Hamburger Day 141
National Kite-Flying Day 140
National Knock-Knock Jokes Day 141
National Lazy Day 141
National Let's Laugh Day 140
National Meteor Watch Day 141
National Mother Goose Day 141
National Pet Day 140
National Play Monopoly Day 141
National Polar Bear Day 140
National Popcorn Day 140
National Random Acts of Kindness Day 140
National Read a Book Day 141
National Reptile Awareness

Day 141
National Saxophone Day 141
National Say Something Nice Day 141
National School Librarian Day 140
National Sock Day 140, 141
National Strawberry Shortcake Day 141
National Take a Hike Day 141
National Tortilla Chip Day 140
National Vanilla Cupcake Day 141
National Violin Day 141
National Wiggle Your Toes Day 141
navigational chart 99
Nazca 68
Nazca lines of Peru 68
N'Dour, Youssou 121
negative geoglyph 68
nepenthes 37
Neptune 11, 20
nerve 58
Netherlands 107, 134, 177
neuron 48
New Delhi 144
Newton, Sir Isaac 62
New York 72, 73, 77, 82, 86, 116, 128, 135, 136, 170
New York Easter Parade 128
nickelodeon 130
"nomophobic" person 95
North American pitcher plant 37
Novak 157
nuclear reactor 63
nucleus 9
nyctophobia 160

O
octopus 35, 40, 53
O'Keeffe, Georgia 116
Olympic Games 199
onion 174
ophidiophobia 161
Oracle Chamber 69
ostrich 60
outer core 17
outer space 215
oxymoron 155

P
Pacific viperfish 30
pack 115, 162
palindrome 155
Palm Jumeirah 74
Pan-American Highway 77
Papua New Guinea 107, 147
paresthesia 149
Paris 73, 86
park 138
Parmesan cheese 183
parrot 44
pasta 178
Pearl Bridge 81
pediophobia 161
Pennsylvania 130
pepper 181
Persia 111
personal computer 93
Peru 68, 107, 110, 169
Peter Rabbit 193
Peters projection 101
phloem bundle 148
phonogram 153
photosphere 9
Picasso, Pablo 119
pigpen cipher 150
pineapple 175
Pink Ribbon Foundation 134
Pink Running Day 134
pitcher plant 37
pizza 184
plane 86, 87, 99, 209
plasma 53
Play-Doh® 189
pod 82, 169
podcar 82
pointe shoe 137
Pointillism 119
polo 197, 202, 203
Pompeii worm 25
Pont du Gard Aqueduct 81
popcorn 169, 179
porridge 177
portable computer 93
Portuguese 147
potato 174
Potter, Beatrix 192
practical steam engine 213
prairie dog 44
precipitation 15
President Abraham Lincoln's stovepipe hat 129
pretzels 169
probability 206
prunes 175
pumpkin regatta 204
puzzles 190
Pygmalion's Spectacles 131
Pyramid of Cheops 73

Q
qabaqib 127
Quebec 132
quiz 189

R
racing cyclist 210
racing pigeon 209
radiation 17, 25, 55, 65
radio show 131
raisins 175
rebus 154
red blood cell 48
Red Planet 10, 20, 96
Rhode Island 159
road 76, 99, 111, 127, 211
road map 99
robot 21, 96, 97
robot vacuum cleaner 97
rock-paper-scissors 199
roller coaster 138
Roman Empire 76, 81
romp 162
Röntgen, Wilhelm 62
Roosevelt, Teddy 192
Rose, Alexander 123
Rosetta (Rashid) 153
Rosetta Stone 153
Rossi 157
Royal Gorge Bridge 81
Rubik's® Cube 189
ruby-red slippers 127
Russia 79, 106, 107, 134, 204, 205

S
saffron 181
Sagrada Familia 75
saliva 47
sarracenia 37
satellite 21, 23, 99
satellite photo 99
Saturn 11, 20, 64
Sauvage, Jean-Pierre 63
Sawyer 156, 165
scallop 32
school 65, 162
science and technology history 63
scientist 12, 65, 66, 78, 88, 97, 146, 151
Scotland 185
Scoville Heat Index 166
Scoville Heat Units 166
Scoville, Wilbur 166
scurry 162
sea otter 67
Senegal 107, 121
senet 130
sensors 59
Seurat, Georges-Pierre 119
Shakespeare, William 28, 159
shift cipher 151
shoe 126, 127, 137
shoe size 126
shuttlecock 201
Silk Road 111
Sistine Chapel 116
skeleton 50
skin 39, 47, 48, 54, 55, 57, 183
skin cell 48
skydiver 208
skyscraper 72
sloth 162
small intestine 47
Smith 157
Smithsonian's National Museum of American History 127
snail 33, 210
snap trap 37
sneaker 126
snowshoe 127
soccer 196, 197, 201, 204
solar eclipse 12
solar power 84
solar roof panel 84
Southern Cross 103
South Korea 103, 107, 185
space junk 22, 23
space suit 90
Space Surveillance Network 22
space trash 23
Spanish 110, 112, 147
speed 58, 60, 82, 85, 113, 208, 211
sperm whale 41
spices 180
spider 31, 53
spiral galaxy 7
Spirit of Freedom balloon 88
Spirit of St. Louis 86
spoonerism 154
sport 131, 196, 197, 198, 202, 204

INDEX

Sputnik 20, 22
squid 53
SR-71 Blackbird 209
standard unit blocks 195
stapes bone 51
starfish 41
static electricity 62
Statue of Liberty 217
steam-driven turbine 66
steam power 66
steam turbine 66
Stegosaurus 212
Steiff 192
stem cell 48
Stoddart, Fraser 63
stonefish 34
stovepipe hat 129
strawberry 174
street map 99
stuffed animals 192
subway 83, 99
subway map 99
Sulabh International Museum of Toilets 144
Sulawesi, Indonesia 114
Sullivan, Roy 206
Sun 6, 9, 10, 11, 12, 84, 214, 216
sundew 36
sunspots 9
surfboard 198
surname 156
Surrealism 118
survival suit 90
swarm 162
Sweden 107, 164
sweet bell pepper 167
Sydney Opera House 74
symbol 103, 111, 142, 149
systems 46, 58, 82, 152

T

table tennis 201
tabula 190
Taglioni, Marie 137
Talk Like a Pirate Day 141
tap dancing 137
tardigrade 25
teapot house 71
teddy bear 192
telescope 7, 64, 65
television 131
temperature 9, 214
temperature at which water boils 214
temperature of Earth's core 215
temperature of molten lava 214
temperature of outer space 215
temperature of Venus 215
temple 69, 103, 111
tennis 197, 200, 203
terrestrial planet 10
Tesla, Nikola 62
Thales of Miletus 62
Thebes 111
thematic map 99
theme park 138
tic-tac-toe cipher 150
tide 12
Tigris 110
titan beetle 43
tittle 149
Tom Swifty 155
tongue print 47
tool 66, 67, 153
Toprock 136
toque 129
toy 188, 189
train 82, 83, 99
train map 99
train platform 83
transistor 67
transportation system 99
Trans-Siberian Railway 82
treadmill 198
Tripitaka tablets 165
triskaidekaphobia 160
troop 162
trypanophobia 161
tsundoku 165
Tube, The 83
tuna 61
Turkey 105, 107, 136, 185
Tyrannosaurus 212

U

Uffington, England 69
Uffington White Horse 69
Ulm Minster 73
uncommon words 148
unit blocks 195
United States 77, 81, 82, 84, 86, 103, 105, 106, 107, 108, 112, 128, 131, 146, 159, 160, 189, 191, 192, 194, 204
universe 7, 65, 212
University of Nebraska-Lincoln 109
upside-down home 71
Uranus 11, 20

V

Van Gogh, Vincent 116
vanilla 180
Vatican City 106, 107
vegetable 174
venom 34
Venus 10, 12, 20, 37, 215
Venus flytrap 37
vertebrate 51
Vienna Vegetable Orchestra 123
Viking 1 20
Viking 2 20
virtual reality 131
virus 65
volcano explorer 91
volleyball 197
Volta, Alessandro 62
Voyager 1 21
Voyager 2 20

W

Walking House 70
Wallace's flying frog 39
Wang 156
Washington, George 29, 139
Wasik, Bill 135
water 10, 14, 15, 17, 20, 25, 38, 39, 53, 58, 79, 81, 91, 103, 117, 118, 128, 132, 135, 140, 166, 202, 205, 208, 214
water bear 25
water polo 202
waterwheel plant 37
weather balloon 208
weaverbird 44
Weinbaum, Stanley G. 131
Wellington, New Zealand 113
whale 61, 77, 163
wheel of law 103
Willie Man-Chew 142
Wisconsin State Cow-Chip Throw 143
wolffish 30
Wolof 121
wooden blocks 194
Wooden Library 164
wood frog 25
word 44, 45, 123, 148, 154, 155, 158, 159, 189
World Animal Day 141
World Braille Day 140
World Frog Day 140
World Lizard Day 141
World Ocean Day 141
World Penguin Day 140
World Population Day 141
World Snake Day 141
World Television Day 141
World Thinking Day 140
World Turtle Day 141
World War I 109, 124
World Water Day 140
World Wide Web 63, 212
Wozniak, Steve 63
Wright brothers 209, 212
Wright brothers' first flight 212
Wright Flyer 86, 209
Wright, Orville 86
Wright, Wilbur 86

X

Xing, Yi 62
X-ray 62

Y

Yap 104
Yi Peng Lantern Festival 142
yo-yo 189

Z

Zanzibar 169
Zimbabwe 105, 107

CREDITS

For each page, photo credits are listed from left to right.

Front Cover: baramee2554/istock/Getty Images
Back Cover: GlobalP/istock/Getty Images
Back Cover: mrsixinthemix/istock/Getty Images
Back Cover: Antagain/istock/Getty Images
2: anna1311/istock/Getty Images
2: avidcreative/istock/Getty Images
2: jondpatton/istock/Getty Images
2: sibrikov/istock/Getty Images
3: koya79/istock/Getty Images
3: AntonMatveev/istock/Getty Images
3: amriphoto/istock/Getty Images
4: alxpin/istock/Getty Images
4: RichLegg/istock/Getty Images
4: leonello/istock/Getty Images
5: Antagain/istock/Getty Images
5: Public Domain
5: ScrappinStacy/istock/Getty Images
5: londoneye/istock/Getty Images
5: joggiebotma/istock/Getty Images
6: alex-mit/iStock/Getty Images
7: European Space Agency & NASA
7: NASA
7: NASA
7: NASA
7: NASA/Marshall Space Flight Center
8: adventtr/iStock/Getty Images
9: NASA/© NASA/SDO/HMI
11: Aphelleon/iStock/Getty Images
11: everlite/iStock/Getty Images
12: Oktay Ortakcioglu/iStock/Getty Images
12: stevecoleimages/iStock/Getty Images
13: spooh/iStock/Getty Images
13: onfokus/iStock/Getty Images
15: SamBurt/iStock/Getty Images
15: posteriori/iStock/Getty Images
15: jack0m /iStock/Getty Images
15: RomoloTavani/iStock/Getty Images
15: Artem_Egorov/iStock/Getty Images
16: adventtr/iStock/Getty Images
17: titoOnz/iStock/Getty Images
18: YinYang/iStock/Getty Images
18: PytyCzech/iStock/Getty Images
19: powerofforever/iStock/Getty Images
19: Elenarts/iStock/Getty Images
20: NASA
20: NASA
20: gremlin/iStock/Getty Images
20: Aunt_Spray/iStock/Getty Images
20: NASA
20: NASA
20: 3DSculptor/iStock/Getty Images
21: NASA
21: inhauscreative/iStock/Getty Images
22: johan63/iStock/Getty Images
22: United States Missile Defense Agency
23: Ania/iStock/Getty Images
23: Petrovich9/iStock/Getty Images
23: 3DSculptor/iStock/Getty Images
24: ultrapro/iStock/Getty Images
24: sbayram/iStock/Getty Images
25: National Science Foundation
25: Eraxion/iStock/Getty Images
25: Rkitki/CC BY 3.0
25: MarkMirror/iStock/Getty Images
26: Global_Pics/iStock/Getty Images
27: Oleandra9/iStock/Getty Images
27: traceyd22/iStock/Getty Images
27: saiko3p/iStock/Getty Images
27: vladvvm/iStock/Getty Images
28: Vichai/iStock/Getty Images
28: thawornnurak/iStock/Getty Images
28: ivan-96/iStock/Getty Images
28: duncan1890/iStock/Getty Images
29: HAKINMHAN/iStock/Getty Images
29: nicoolay/iStock/Getty Images
29: traveler1116/iStock/Getty Images
29: Doug Bray/istock/Getty Images
29: peepo//iStock/Getty Images
30: Hailshadow/iStock/Getty Images
30: demarfa/iStock/Getty Images
30: kickers/iStock/Getty Images
30: David Csepp/NOAA
31: Public Domain
31: NOAA
31: pr2is/iStock/Getty Images
31: Javontaevious/CC BY SA-3.0
32: alexnika/iStock/Getty Images
32: Brufal/iStock/Getty Images
32: ShaneKato/iStock/Getty Images
33: Freder/iStock/Getty Images
33: imv/iStock/Getty Images
33: ConstantinCornel/iStock/Getty Images
33: EcoPic/iStock/Getty Images
34: wrangel/iStock/Getty Images
34: ~UserGI15667539/iStock/Getty Images
34: zentilia/iStock/Getty Images
34: RibeirodosSantos/iStock/Getty Images
34: Alastair Rae/CC BY-SA 2.0
35: davidevison/iStock/Getty Images
36: Tailex/iStock/Getty Images
37: Jan Wleneke/CC BY-SA 3.0
37: AlessandroZocc/iStock/Getty Images
37: kritsada171/iStock/Getty Images
37: KT_PARK/iStock/Getty Images
38: ANDREYGUDKOV/iStock/Getty Images
39: Manojiritty/CC BY 4.0
39: common_human/iStock/Getty Images
39: mdurstewitz/iStock/Getty Images
39: shabeerthurakkal/iStock/Getty Images
40: Antagain/iStock/Getty Images
40: shaunl/iStock/Getty Images
41: pixelprof/iStock/Getty Images
41: LagunaticPhoto/iStock/Getty Images
41: KenCanning/iStock/Getty Images
41: wombatzaa/iStock/Getty Images
41: ShaneGross/iStock/Getty Images
42: SHAWSHANK61/iStock/Getty Images
42: Dodoni/CC BY 3.0
43: fotolinchen/iStock/Getty Images
43: nikpal/iStock/Getty Images
43: Paolo_Toffanin/iStock/Getty Images
43: gprentice/iStock/Getty Images
44: allgord/iStock/Getty Images
44: Binty/iStock/Getty Images
44: Utopia_88/iStock/Getty Images
44: jarenwicklund/iStock/Getty Images
44: Brian_D_Watters/iStock/Getty Images
44: BraunS/iStock/Getty Images
44: swissmediavision/iStock/Getty Images
45: RichVintage/iStock/Getty Images
46: yodiyim/iStock/Getty Images
46: huronphoto/iStock/Getty Images
46: liza5450/iStock/Getty Images
47: VolodymyrV/iStock/Getty Images
47: ellobo1/iStock/Getty Images
47: scanrail/iStock/Getty Images
47: MichaelJay/iStock/Getty Images
47: Nerthuz/iStock/Getty Images
47: Yuri_Arcurs/iStock/Getty Images
47: AWelshLad/iStock/Getty Images
47: RuslanDashinsky/iStock/Getty Images
48: Henrik5000/iStock/Getty Images
48: Christogra4/iStock/Getty Images
48: Image Source/iStock/Getty Images
48: PhonlamaiPhoto/iStock/Getty Images
48: luismmolina/iStock/Getty Images
48: Johanna Poetsch/iStock/Getty Images
48: Henrik5000/iStock/Getty Images
49: Jorge Villalba/iStock/Getty Images
49: ClPhotos/iStock/Getty Images
49: iLexx/iStock/Getty Images
49: gremlin/iStock/Getty Images
50: diane39/iStock/Getty Images
50: Alija/iStock/Getty Images
51: Welleschik/CC BY 3.0
51: Eraxion/iStock/Getty Images
51: real444/iStock/Getty Images
51: yodiyim/iStock/Getty Images
51: Eraxion/iStock/Getty Images
52: sankalpmaya/iStock/Getty Images x
52: Halfpoint/iStock/Getty Images
52: Gannet77/iStock/Getty Images
52: baona/iStock/Getty Images
52: adventtr/iStock/Getty Images
53: Freder/iStock/Getty Images
53: PaulFleet/iStock/Getty Images
53: farakos/iStock/Getty Images
53: wrangel/iStock/Getty Images
53: valentinrussanov/iStock/Getty Images
54: RusN/iStock/Getty Images
54: PenelopeB/iStock/Getty Images
54: ttsz/iStock/Getty Images
54: VolodymyrV/iStock/Getty Images
55: PeopleImages/iStock/Getty Images
55: man_at_mouse/iStock/Getty Images
56: Vizerskaya/iStock/Getty Images
56: mraoraor/iStock/Getty Images
56: art-4-art/iStock/Getty Images
56: Yulia-Images/iStock/Getty Images
56: inarik/iStock/Getty Images
57: llhedgehogll/iStock/Getty Images
57: claire222/iStock/Getty Images
57: Eivaisla/iStock/Getty Images
57: 4FR/iStock/Getty Images
57: Tverdohlib/iStock/Getty Images
57: Weekend Images Inc./iStock/Getty Images
58: Rost-9D/iStock/Getty Images
58: BlackJack3D/iStock/Getty Images
58: adventtr/iStock/Getty Images
58: Peopleimages/iStock/Getty Images
58: rosliothman/iStock/Getty Images
58: iLexx/iStock/Getty Images
59: yodiyim/iStock/Getty Images
59: Firstsignal/iStock/Getty Images
60: JohnCarnemolla/iStock/Getty Images
60: Dmytro Aksonov/iStock/Getty Images
60: BraunS/iStock/Getty Images
60: olga_gl/iStock/Getty Images
61: takoburito/iStock/Getty Images
61: Ljupco/iStock/Getty Images
61: MaFelipe/iStock/Getty Images
61: Tomwang112/iStock/Getty Images
61: miblue5/iStock/Getty Images
61: ElisaGH/iStock/Getty Images
62: RichVintage/iStock/Getty Images
62: lucentius/iStock/Getty Images
62: Lautam17/CC BY-SA 3.0
62: traveler1116/iStock/Getty Images
62: belterz/iStock/Getty Images
62: Public Domain
63: Melvin A. Miller/U.S. Department of Energy
63: 100pk/iStock/Getty Images
63: gecko753/iStock/Getty Images
64: jamesbenet/iStock/Getty Images
64: richcano/iStock/Getty Images
64: yipengge/iStock/Getty Images
66: DGerriePhotography/iStock/Getty Images
66: Goldcastle7/iStock/Getty Images
66: sspopov/iStock/Getty Images
67: Wlad74/iStock/Getty Images
67: sibrikov/iStock/Getty Images
67: thomaslenne/iStock/Getty Images
68: ArtMarie/iStock/Getty Images
69: Peulle/CC BY-SA 4.0
69: JohnnyGreig/iStock/Getty Images
69: Hamelin de Guettelet/CC BY-SA 3.0
70: IvanMiladinovic/iStock/Getty Images
70: Rainer Halama/CC BY-SA 3.0
70: Grigur/CC BY-SA 4.0
71: backkratze/CC BY 2.0
71: Steven & Nadine Pavlov/CC BY-SA 3.0
72: dblight/iStock/Getty Images
72: stbaus7/iStock/Getty Images
73: Lindrik/iStock/Getty Images
73: wdstock/iStock/Getty Images
73: LiliGraphie/iStock/Getty Images
73: klug-photo/iStock/Getty Images
74: drawdrawdraw/iStock/Getty Images
74: Mlenny/iStock/Getty Images
75: dem10/iStock/Getty Images
75: Dicklyon/CC BY-SA 4.0
76: kevron2001/iStock/Getty Images
76: Sean_Warren/iStock/Getty Images
76: wabeno/iStock/Getty Images
76: valio84sl/iStock/Getty Images
77: caseyimage/iStock/Getty Images
77: Lenorlux/iStock/Getty Images
77: StockPhotosArt/iStock/Getty Images
78: real444/iStock/Getty Images
79: Joesboy/iStock/Getty Images
79: Andre Belozeroff/CC BY-SA 3.0
79: Pavliha/iStock/Getty Images
79: frentusha/iStock/Getty Images
79: evenfh/iStock/Getty Images
79: Robin_Hoood/iStock/Getty Images
80: espiegle/iStock/Getty Images
80: crazlei/CC BY-SA 2.0
80: Oktay Ortakcioglu/iStock/Getty Images
81: jsteck/iStock/Getty Images
81: guenterguni/iStock/Getty Images
81: pranodhm/iStock/Getty Images
82: Yongyuan Dai/iStock/Getty Images
82: rutin55/iStock/Getty Images
82: Skybum/CC BY 3.0
82: paylessimages/iStock/Getty Images
83: chris55/CC BY-SA 3.0
83: MarioGuti/iStock/Getty Images
84: Nerthuz/iStock/Getty Images
84: DaimlerChrysler AG/CC BY-SA 3.0
84: koya79/iStock/Getty Images
84: baileystock/iStock/Getty Images
85: mevans/iStock/Getty Images
86: Raul654/CC BY-SA 3.0
86: IFCAR/CC BY-SA 3.0
86: asmithers/iStock/Getty Images
86: John T. Daniels/Public Domain
86: Nigel Coates/CC BY-SA 3.0
87: Kristen Terrana-Hollis
88: artpritsadee/iStock/Getty Images
88: By Sam Shere [No restrictions] via Wikimedia Commons
88: popovaphoto/iStock/Getty Images
88: AdventurePicture/iStock/Getty Images
88: United States Missile Defense Agency/Public Domain
88: TONY ASHBY/Stringer/AFP/Getty Images
89: luismmolina/iStock/Getty Images
90: flyparade/iStock/Getty Images
90: Aaron Ansarov/U.S. NAVY
90: lexaarts/iStock/Getty Images
91: Leeuwtje/iStock/Getty Images
91: zhaubasar/iStock/Getty Images
91: superwebdeveloper/CC BY 2.0
92: Andrew Dunn/CC BY 2.0
92: U.S. Army/Public Domain
93: Maxiphoto/iStock/Getty Images
93: Adam Jenkins/CC BY 3.0
93: LDProd/iStock/Getty Images
93: freemixer/iStock/Getty Images
94: olaser/iStock/Getty Images
94: filadendron/iStock/Getty Images
94: Rico Shen/CC BY-SA 3.0
94: AlexRaths/iStock/Getty Images
95: GlobalStock/iStock/Getty Images
95: Art-Of-Photo/iStock/Getty Images
96: Chesky_W/iStock/Getty Images
96: NASA
97: mennovandijk/iStock/Getty Images
97: coffeekai/iStock/Getty Images
97: koya79/iStock/Getty Images
97: canakat/iStock/Getty Images
98: AWSeebaran/iStock/Getty Images
99: Yuri_Arcurs/iStock/Getty Images
99: alexsl/iStock/Getty Images
99: gio_bamfi/iStock/Getty Images
99: U.S. Navy/Public Domain
99: seamartini/iStock/Getty Images
99: DieterMeyrl/iStock/Getty Images
101: Milan_Jovic/iStock/Getty Images
101: NASA
101: NASA
102: Rawpixel/iStock/Getty Images
103: spawns/iStock/Getty Images
103: ronniechua/iStock/Getty Images
103: daboost/iStock/Getty Images
103: daboost/iStock/Getty Images
103: shaadjutt/iStock/Getty Images
103: ronniechua/iStock/Getty Images
103: sitox/iStock/Getty Images
103: daboost/istock/Getty Images
103: shaadjutt/istock/Getty Images
104: baona/istock/Getty Images
104: Peter2pan/CC BY-SA 3.0
105: YinYang/istock/Getty Images
105: oversnap/istock/Getty Images
105: andresr/istock/Getty Images
105: robstyle/istock/Getty Images
106: kosmozoo/istock/Getty Images
108: Viatcheslav/istock/Getty Images
108: WilshireImages/istock/Getty Images
109: Sandstein/CC BY-SA 3.0
109: g-stockstudio/istock/Getty Images
109: skodonnell/istock/Getty Images
109: cmannphoto/istock/Getty Images
110: Siempreverde22/istock/Getty Images
110: KeithBinns/istock/Getty Images
111: HomoCosmicos/istock/Getty Images
111: Maxiphoto/istock/Getty Images
111: Elnur/istock/Getty Images
112: saiko3p/istock/Getty Images
112: Aivita/istock/Getty Images
113: ArtoMagicman/istock/Getty Images
113: Danielrao/istock/Getty Images
113: eikrid/istock/Getty Images
114: Thoams T./CC BY-SA 2.0
115: Rameessos/Public Domain
115: HTO/Public Domain
116: Public Domain
116: dbvirago/istock/Getty Images
116: Public Domain
117: Public Domain
117: Public Domain
118: Public Domain
118: Bettmann/Bettmann Archive/Getty Images
118: Public Domain
118: Public Domain
119: Public Domain
119: Universal History Archive/UIG/Getty Images
119: Public Domain
119: Public Domain
120: Zhenikeyev/istock/Getty Images
120: 200mm/istock/Getty Images
121: Thesupermat/CC BY-SA 3.0
121: MarkRubens/istock/Getty Images
121: akinbostanci/istock/Getty Images
122: fisher_photostudio/istock/Getty Images
122: abluecup/istock/Getty Images
123: ClaudioValdes/istock/Getty Images
123: vu3kkm/istock/Getty Images
123: VickyRu/istock/Getty Images
124: Bepsimage/istock/Getty Images
124: ratpack223/istock/Getty Images
124: zoranm/istock/Getty Images
124: Library of Congress/Public Domain
125: maxphotography/istock/Getty Images
125: Jason_V/istock/Getty Images
125: liquid_image/istock/Getty Images
125: FatCamera/istock/Getty Images
126: guenterguni/istock/Getty Images
127: NASA
127: dbking/CC BY 2.0
127: Olivier Blondeau/istock/Getty Images
127: Northampton Museum/CC BY 2.0

CREDITS

128: Jarp/istock/Getty Images
128: vm/istock/Getty Images
128: TD Dolci/istock/Getty Images
128: Sam Edwards/istock/Getty Images
129: Erstudiostok/istock/Getty Images
129: Smithsonian/Public Domain
129: TimJN1 Bradshaw/CC BY-SA 2.0
130: Maxiphoto/istock/Getty Images
130: BabelStone/Public Domain
130: William James/Public Domain
130: Charles Edwin Wilbour Fund/ Brooklyn Museum
131: ABC Television/Public Domain
132: Didier Messens/Getty Images Entertainment/Getty Images
132: McManus-Young Collection/ Public Domain
133: AntGor/istock/Getty Images
133: cliff1066™/CC BY 2.0
134: Berkut_34/istock/Getty Images
134: TonyTaylorStock/istock/Getty Images
135: Liz Leyden/istock/Getty Images
135: OcusFocus/istock/Getty Images
137: oneinchpunch/istock/Getty Images
137: ferrantraite/istock/Getty Images
137: joshblake/istock/Getty Images
137: toxawww/istock/Getty Images
137: LdF/istock/Getty Images
138: sihasakprachum/istock/Getty Images
138: Christian Mueller/istock/ Getty Images
139: Igal6/istock/Getty Images
139: Nikada/istock/Getty Images
139: mf-guddyx/istock/Getty Images
140: RichLegg/istock/Getty Images
140: HowardPerry/istock/Getty Images
140: luiscarlosjimenez/istock/ Getty Images
140: Image Source/istock/Getty Images
140: asiseeit/istock/Getty Images
141: Magone/istock/Getty Images
141: dbvirago/istock/Getty Images
141: Zheka-Boss/istock/Getty Images
141: Rawpixel/istock/Getty Images
141: sveta_zarzamora/istock/ Getty Images
141: lucop/istock/Getty Images
141: aabejon/istock/Getty Images
141: 2thirdsphoto/istock/Getty Images
141: KQconcepts/istock/Getty Images
142: tropper2000/istock/Getty Images
142: ConstantinCornel/istock/ Getty Images
143: FatManPhotoUK/istock/Getty Images
143: By tooguether/CC BY-SA 3.0
143: Berezko/istock/Getty Images
144: fstop123/istock/Getty Images
145: Suradech14/istock/Getty Images
145: WichitS/istock/Getty Images
145: Russ Bowling/CC BY-SA 4.0
145: Davidmerkoski/CC BY 2.0
146: kiankhoon/istock/Getty Images
146: mrPliskin/istock/Getty Images
146: GCShutter/istock/Getty Images
147: kgtoh/istock/Getty Images
147: kiankhoon/istock/Getty Images
147: Byelikova_Oksana/istock/ Getty Images
148: LeventKonuk/istock/Getty Images
148: Marco Rosario Venturini Autieri/ istock/Getty Images
148: Antagain/istock/Getty Images
149: ISerg/istock/Getty Images
149: Magone/istock/Getty Images
149: gangliu10/istock/Getty Images
149: ekremguduk/istock/Getty Images
149: whitemay/istock/Getty Images
149: crisserbug/istock/Getty Images
149: Wylius/istock/Getty Images
149: Wylius/istock/Getty Images
149: Wylius/istock/Getty Images
150: excentric_01/istock/Getty Images
151: JRLPhotographer/istock/ Getty Images
151: Austin Mills/CC BY-SA 3.0
151: PeterAustin/istock/Getty Images
152: swisshippo/istock/Getty Images
152: jordifa/istock/Getty Images
153: paylessimages/istock/Getty Images
153: nicomenijes/istock/Getty Images
153: AmandaLewis/istock/Getty Images
154: sureshsharma/istock/Getty Images
154: Spauln/istock/Getty Images
154: Anetlanda/istock/Getty Images
154: Wavebreakmedia/istock/ Getty Images
154: SvetlanaK/istock/Getty Images
155: MikeSPb/istock/Getty Images
155: jenifoto/istock/Getty Images
155: Pepgooner/istock/Getty Images
156: izusek/istock/Getty Images
156: LeonidKos/istock/Getty Images
156: EHStock/istock/Getty Images/Vetta
156: michaelztong/istock/Getty Images
156: StockFinland/istock/Getty Images
157: redmal/istock/Getty Images
157: urfinguss/istock/Getty Images
157: igorr1/istock/Getty Images
157: Vesnaandjic/istock/Getty Images
157: woolzian/istock/Getty Images
158: joey333/istock/Getty Images
158: monkeybusinessimages/istock/ Getty Images
159: Tolga TEZCAN/CC BY-SA 3.0
159: dk_photos/istock/Getty Images
160: Photobuff/istock/Getty Images
161: miqul/istock/Getty Images
161: miljko/istock/Getty Images
161: kavring/istock/Getty Images
161: joakimbkk/istock/Getty Images
161: brazzo/istock/Getty Images
161: DNY59/istock/Getty Images
161: Motizova/istock/Getty Images
162: Pierrot46/istock/Getty Images
162: bazilfoto/istock/Getty Images
162: AntonMatveev/istock/Getty Images
162: A330Pilot/istock/Getty Images
163: eco2drew/istock/Getty Images
163: mediaphotos/istock/Getty Images
163: VisualCommunications/istock/ Getty Images
163: CraigRJD/istock/Getty Images
164: blackred/istock/Getty Images
164: Haeferl/CC BY-SA 3.0
165: georgeclerk/istock/Getty Images
165: Thierry Falise/LightRocket/ Getty Images
166: DrPAS/istock/Getty Images
166: dra_schwartz/istock/Getty Images
166: ZoneCreative/istock/Getty Images
167: maxsol7/istock/Getty Images
167: skrip/istock/Getty Images
167: DNY59/istock/Getty Images
167: DrPAS/istock/Getty Images
167: mrsixinthemix/istock/Getty Images
167: shell125/istock/Getty Images
167: Tree4Two/istock/Getty Images
167: vitalsss/istock/Getty Images
167: Suzifoo/istock/Getty Images
167: eli_asenova/istock/Getty Images
168: etiennevoss/istock/Getty Images
168: emptyclouds/istock/Getty Images
169: PicturePartners/istock/Getty Images
169: Jamesmcq24/istock/Getty Images
169: MarkGillow/istock/Getty Images
169: John Sommer/istock/Getty Images
169: EddWestmacott/istock/Getty Images
169: kaanates/istock/Getty Images
169: kaanates/istock/Getty Images
170: anna1311/istock/Getty Images
170: artiss/istock/Getty Images
170: wundervisuals/istock/Getty Images
171: michellegibson/istock/Getty Images
172: MillefloreImages/istock/Getty Images
172: TheCrimsonMonkey/istock/ Getty Images
172: hiramtom/istock/Getty Images
173: Clicknique/istock/Getty Images
173: max-kegfire/istock/Getty Images
173: Floortje/istock/Getty Images
173: ScrappinStacy/istock/Getty Images
174: Grafner/istock/Getty Images
174: Natikka kaanates real444/istock/ Getty Images
174: Natikka/istock/Getty Images
174: shaun/istock/Getty Images
175: kertlis/istock/Getty Images
175: eyewave/istock/Getty Images
175: popovaphoto/istock/Getty Images
175: Frantysek/istock/Getty Images
175: Valengilda/istock/Getty Images
175: MariaBrzostowska/istock/ Getty Images
176: kiboka/istock/Getty Images
176: gojak/istock/Getty Images
177: sara_winter/istock/Getty Images
177: PetrMalyshev/istock/Getty Images
177: Magone/istock/Getty Images
178: zhekos/istock/Getty Images
178: egal/istock/Getty Images
178: Elenathewise/istock/Getty Images
178: Floortje/istock/Getty Images
179: eyewave/istock/Getty Images
179: MariusLtu/istock/Getty Images
179: enviromantic/istock/Getty Images
179: TheCrimsonMonkey/istock/ Getty Images
179: DGArtes/istock/Getty Images
180: Nataliia_Pyzhova/istock/ Getty Images
180: KMNPhoto/istock/Getty Images
180: naruedom/istock/Getty Images
180: Ockra/istock/Getty Images
180: ClaudioStocco/istock/Getty Images
181: Nataliia_Pyzhova/istock/ Getty Images
181: chfonk/istock/Getty Images
181: nito100/istock/Getty Images
181: kcline/istock/Getty Images
181: AtnoYdur/istock/Getty Images
181: Elenathewise/istock/Getty Images
182: ChiccoDodiFC/istock/Getty Images
182: barbaraaaa/istock/Getty Images
182: Magone/istock/Getty Images
183: lizzyhayman/istock/Getty Images
183: AlasdairJames/istock/Getty Images
183: vusta/istock/Getty Images
183: Andrew McMillan/CC BY
183: GlobalP/istock/Getty Images
183: ac_bnphotos/istock/Getty Images
183: ipag/istock/Getty Images
183: Tsekhmister/istock/Getty Images
184: Barcin/istock/Getty Images
185: NZSteve/istock/Getty Images
185: skyjo/istock/Getty Images
185: margouillatphotos/istock/ Getty Images
185: alpaksoy/istock/Getty Images
185: Pichunter/istock/Getty Images
185: Independent Picture Service/ Universal Images Group/ Getty Images
186: LauriPatterson/istock/Getty Images
186: HighImpactPhotography/istock/ Getty Images
186: nilsz/istock/Getty Images
186: Elenathewise/istock/Getty Images
187: carlosalvarez/istock/Getty Images
187: mayakova/istock/Getty Images
187: MorePixels/istock/Getty Images
187: robynmac/istock/Getty Images
187: GMVozd/istock/Getty Images
188: omgimages/istock/Getty Images
188: JB/CC BY-SA 3.0
189: dem10/istock/Getty Images
189: Popartic/istock/Getty Images
189: KateLeigh/istock/Getty Images
189: Blade_kostas/istock/Getty Images
189: Westbury/istock/Getty Images
190: ThomasVogel/istock/Getty Images
190: axelbueckert/istock/Getty Images
190: txking/istock/Getty Images
191: Sezeryadigar/istock/Getty Images
191: DNY59/istock/Getty Images
191: VisionDigital/istock/Getty Images
192: Public Domain
192: LisaValder/istock/Getty Images
192: ivanastar/istock/Getty Images
192: GregChristman/istock/Getty Images
193: ivanastar/istock/Getty Images
193: Choreograph/istock/Getty Images
193: Carl Court/Getty Images News/ Getty Images
194: joji/istock/Getty Images
194: WeMcLaughlins/istock/Getty Images
194: Nenov/istock/Getty Images
194: KariHoglund/istock/Getty Images
195: kyoshino/istock/Getty Images
195: choness/istock/Getty Images
196: Rouzes/istock/Getty Images
196: goir/istock/Getty Images
196: mel-nik/istock/Getty Images
196: peepo/istock/Getty Images
197: ilbusca/istock/Getty Images
197: Viorika/istock/Getty Images
197: EHStock/istock/Getty Images
197: hanzl/istock/Getty Images
197: paylessimages/istock/Getty Images
197: stockcam/istock/Getty Images
197: Willard/istock/Getty Images
197: Nastco/istock/Getty Images
197: FreezingRain/istock/Getty Images
197: walik/istock/Getty Images
197: 36clicks/istock/Getty Images
198: ImageDB/istock/Getty Images
198: Jared Sislin Photography/istock/ Getty Images
198: MichaelSvoboda/istock/Getty Images
199: Johah_H/istock/Getty Images
199: PeskyMonkey/istock/Getty Images
199: Alija/istock/Getty Images
199: combomambo/istock/Getty Images
199: NickyBlade/istock/Getty Images
200: momnjax/istock/Getty Images
200: pagadesign/istock/Getty Images
200: C-You/istock/Getty Images
200: C-You/istock/Getty Images
200: BrianAJackson/istock/Getty Images
200: joebelanger/istock/Getty Images
200: Let-c/istock/Getty Images
200: Photobalance/istock/Getty Images
201: GaryRohman/istock/Getty Images
201: Barcin/istock/Getty Images
201: francisblack/istock/Getty Images
201: Grafner/istock/Getty Images
201: netopaek/istock/Getty Images
201: skodonnell/istock/Getty Images
202: FatCamera/istock/Getty Images
202: arianarama/istock/Getty Images
202: OSTILL/istock/Getty Images
202: ferrantraite/istock/Getty Images
203: Vitality73/istock/Getty Images
203: cmannphoto/istock/Getty Images
203: Willard/istock/Getty Images
203: RichardSchmon/istock/Getty Images
203: amriphoto/istock/Getty Images
203: redmal/istock/Getty Images
204: mountaindweller/istock/Getty Images
204: londoneye/istock/Getty Images
204: samdiesel/istock/Getty Images
204: suesmith2/istock/Getty Images
205: donnichols/istock/Getty Images
205: OSTILL/istock/Getty Images
205: Trevor-Mayes/istock/Getty Images
205: llexImage/istock/Getty Images
205: fakezzz/istock/Getty Images
205: primeimages/istock/Getty Images
205: Bossaball Master/CC BY-SA 4.0
206: scibak/istock/Getty Images
206: jhorrocks/istock/Getty Images
206: ronstik/istock/Getty Images
207: Eugene_Onischenko/istock/ Getty Images
207: AnaBGD/istock/Getty Images
207: johan63/istock/Getty Images
207: cmannphoto/istock/Getty Images
207: Flightlevel80/istock/Getty Images
207: cglade/istock/Getty Images
207: ismagilov/istock/Getty Images
208: joggiebotma/istock/Getty Images
208: tihidon/istock/Getty Images
208: CarGe/istock/Getty Images
208: milehightraveler/istock/Getty Images
208: joggiebotma/istock/Getty Images
208: Massimo Tina Pellicciardi/CC BY 2.0
209: Maxiphoto/istock/Getty Images
209: 3DSculptor/istock/Getty Images
209: Pgiam/istock/Getty Images
209: jondpatton/istock/Getty Images
209: luismmolina/istock/Getty Images
209: suriya silsaksom/istock/ Getty Images
209: malexeum/istock/Getty Images
210: Andrey_Kuzmin/istock/Getty Images
210: Imgorthand/istock/Getty Images
210: rbv/istock/istock/Getty Images
210: fotoVoyager/istock/Getty Images
210: Lepro/istock/Getty Images
210: zokru/istock/Getty Images
210: avid_creative/istock/Getty Images
210: kieferpix/istock/Getty Images
211: cynoclub/istock/Getty Images
211: Henrik5000/istock/Getty Images
211: hxdbzxy/istock/Getty Images
212: janrysavy/istock/Getty Images
212: kevron2001/istock/Getty Images
212: spumador/istock/Getty Images
212: Library of Congress
212: NASA
213: Simon002/istock/Getty Images
213: bravo1954/istock/Getty Images
213: Luije/istock/Getty Images
214: mrtom-uk/istock/Getty Images
214: imaginima/istock/Getty Images
214: PeopleImages/istock/Getty Images
214: Magnascan/istock/Getty Images
214: poweroffforever/istock/Getty Images
215: forplayday/istock/Getty Images
215: sandsun/istock/Getty Images
215: LawrenceSawyer/istock/ Getty Images
215: Nick Dale/istock/Getty Images
215: forplayday/istock/Getty Images
215: parameter/istock/Getty Images
216: scpist/istock/Getty Images
216: 4x6/istock/Getty Images
216: GlobalP/istock/Getty Images
216: Andrey_Kuzmin/istock/Getty Images
216: spinout/istock/Getty Images
216: 3dts/istock/Getty Images
217: eco2drew/istock/Getty Images
217: mehmettorlak/istock/Getty Images
217: RuthBlack/istock/Getty Images
217: MasterLu/istock/Getty Images

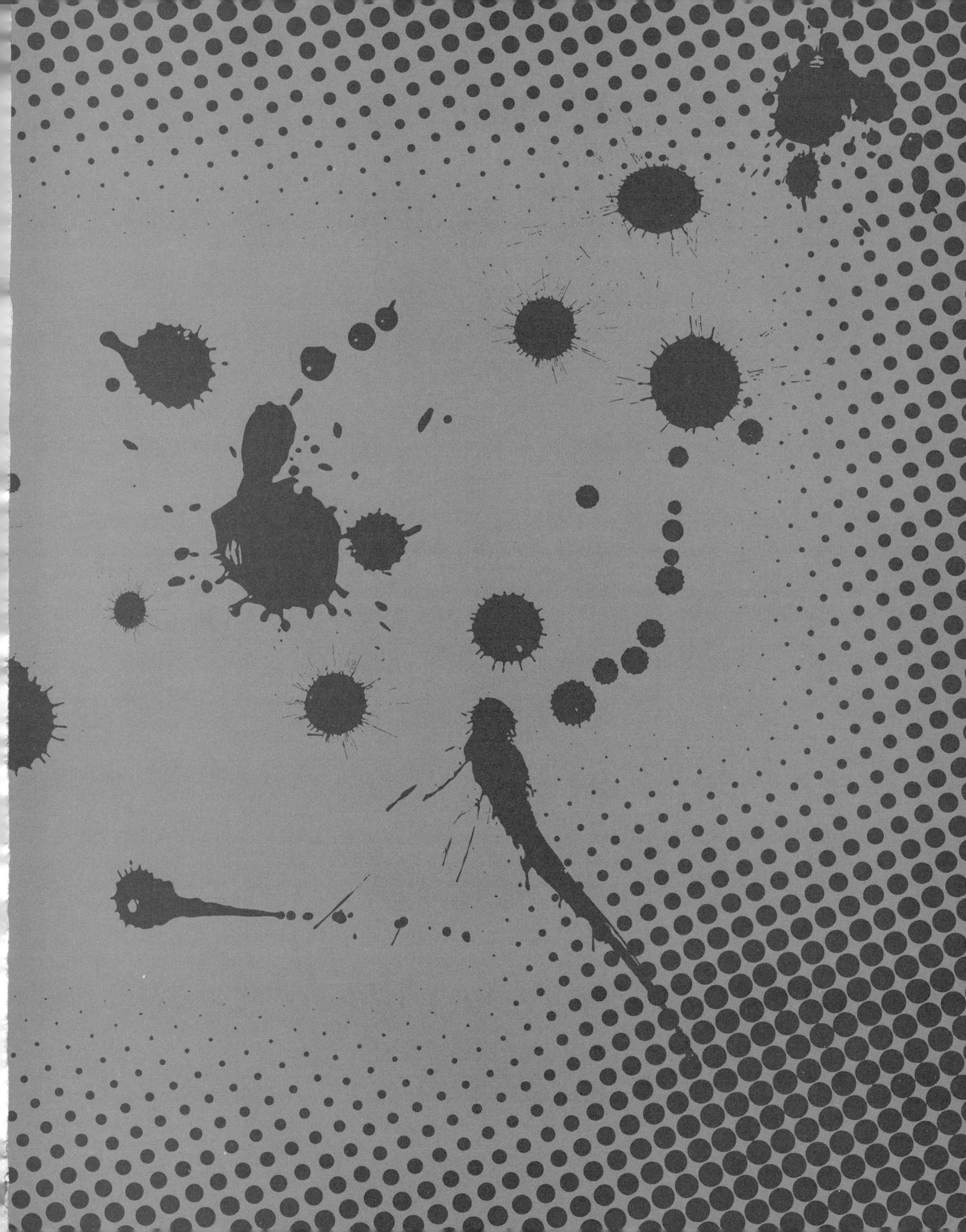

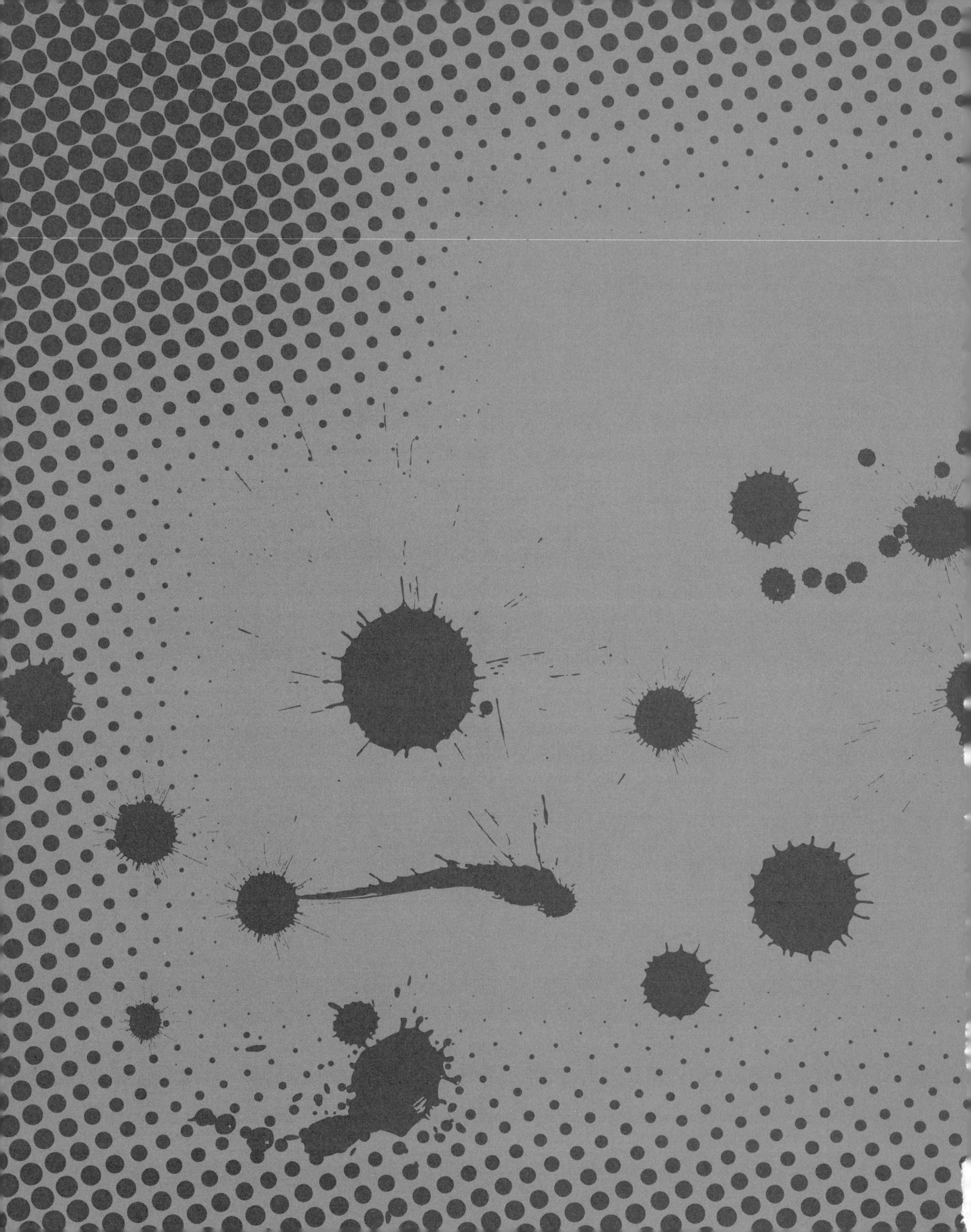